Christmas by the Sea and An Amish Christmas Gift

Christmas by the Sea and An Amish Christmas Gift

Beth Wiseman

THORNDIKE PRESS
A part of Gale, a Cengage Company

Thorndike Press, a part of Gale, a Cengage Company.

Thorndike Press® Large Print Christian Romance.
The text of this Large Print edition is unabridged.
Other aspects of the book may vary from the original edition.
Set in 19 pt. Plantin.

LIBRARY OF CONGRESS CIP DATA ON FILE.
CATALOGUING IN PUBLICATION FOR THIS BOOK
IS AVAILABLE FROM THE LIBRARY OF CONGRESS.

ISBN-13: 978-1-4205-2070-5 (hardcover alk. paper)

Published in 2025 by arrangement with Beth Wiseman.

Printed in the United States of America
1 2 3 4 5 6 7 29 28 27 26 25

▪ ▪ ▪ ▪

Christmas by the Sea

▪ ▪ ▪ ▪

Galveston, Texas . . .

Parker squeezed his eyes closed, the pain in his left leg unbearable, but it was the rising water that slung his mortality around like a slingshot with no aim. Murky floodwaters swirled and collided in organized unison atop his chest. Another three or four inches and the water would be up to his chin.

As rain pelted against his face like rounds of ammunition, Parker gasped for breath in shallow gulps, his faith teetering. He'd been a good Christian his entire life, but as he faced death now, fear and apprehension ruled. Had he really lived as good a life as he could have?

He tried again to move his trapped leg, only to cry out into a weather event that had no mercy, a tropical storm turned hurricane within the past few hours. His sales meeting had run long, and he wondered if his coworkers and friends had managed to get off the island safely. After his car stalled near the cruise terminal, he'd tried to wade to higher ground, but branches and dead tree limbs shared the water with him, and now he was lodged against a concrete pillar, held firmly by a tree branch that crushed his leg in a way that left it feeling numb and detached from his body.

Is this how I will go, God? As a lifelong resident of Galveston Island, the Texas Gulf Coast was as familiar to Parker McIntyre as breathing the briny air. He'd been stung by jellyfish eight times, surfed the tide during past hurricanes, and pulled in a shark on his rod and reel fishing from the jetties. He knew the Historic Strand District by heart and which restaurants were worthy of his hard-earned dollars. And his wife, Cecelia, had birthed their child at John Sealy Hospital four years ago. *Spencer.* His heart ached at the thought of never seeing his son again.

He closed his eyes in prayer again, but even as he tried to focus on communion with God, fear wrapped around him like a serpent squeezing the life out of him. Wondering what it would feel like to drown, he prayed that God would send an angel to help him make the journey. Maybe even Cecelia.

Alex put her car in park on high ground and dialed 9-1-1. She had seen someone's head barely above the water, leaning against a concrete pillar in the distance, as the water rose around the guy. Her heart hammered in her chest as a recorded message played on her cell phone — *all circuits busy.* She knew better than to wade out in water to her chest with all the debris swirling in fast currents around him. Dialing again, she got the same message. As the rain slowed down, she glimpsed the Christmas wreaths in the distance, lit by the grace of God only, since almost every other area had gone dark from the storm. Each year, decorations seemed to go up earlier. It wasn't even Thanksgiving yet. Clenching her cell phone, she blasted herself for not leaving Galveston sooner. Authorities had given ample warnings to vacate the island, but a hurricane in November? She couldn't recall a storm like this in her lifetime so late in the season.

She'd stayed at the hospital longer

than she'd intended, knowing it might be the last time she would see her father. But she had felt that way every day for the past two months after a visit. Sometimes she stayed in her father's room, but she'd forgotten her heart medicine this morning, so she had opted to go home. Missing the meds wouldn't put her health at risk, but her elevated pulse would cause her heart to pound like a base drum in her chest.

Glancing at the man in the water, she walked around to the trunk of her car and searched for a tie strap or bungee cord. She needed something to tie to her car so she could hold onto the other end. If she was going to walk into the floodwaters, she wanted to be able to get back to her car. She wasn't a strong swimmer, and even if she was, the current looked strong enough to sweep her away, a thought that caused her bottom lip to tremble. She wasn't adventuresome by nature, so this potential rescue sent her heart racing even more as she realized the bungee cord she'd found wouldn't be nearly long enough. She tossed it back in the trunk and called 9-1-1 again and jumped when she heard a voice.

"9-1-1. What is your emergency?"

"I'm on Harborside Drive near the cruise terminal, and a man is trapped in the water. It looks like he's pinned against a concrete pillar."

“What is your name, please?”

Alex scowled. “Alex Hansen. Please hurry.”

She paced the length of her car as she detailed her exact location, not taking her eyes off of the man, the water rising to within a few feet of her Honda. If she didn’t move her car soon, she was going to be trapped as well. But she couldn’t leave a man to drown.

As the winds picked up, more branches floated atop the rushing water that separated her and the stranger, and within a few seconds, the downpour resumed. Water was up to the guy’s chin. *Dear Lord, please. What do I do?*

After the 9-1-1 operator came back on the line and said someone was on the way, Alex hit End, tossed the phone on her seat, and locked the car. She opened the door to the gas tank and put her keys inside the compartment before closing it again. Then she took a hesitant step into the water, thankful she'd worn tennis shoes today. The force of the unwelcome seawater gyrated around her ankles, and as she eased forward, it wasn't long before the water was up to her thighs. *Stupid, stupid.* Keeping her eye on the man, while also scanning the area around her, her stomach churned when she thought she saw a snake, but it was only a stick.

With slow steps and sheer will forcing her feet forward, she got within shouting distance of the man, but no matter how much she cried out to him, the wind slammed against her voice, abducting the sound into its wrath. As the guy moved his mouth, she couldn't hear anything he said, but she was within a few yards now, the water to her waist. If she lost her footing, she was going to be swept away. She thought about her father and the irony of the situation if she went before him.

Slow and steady.

The rain eased up again, but the winds fiercely tugged at her, first one way, then the other. She'd lived in Galveston long enough to know how fast the water could rise, so she picked up her pace, trembling but determined.

Her father's strong will and perseverance leapt into the forefront of her mind as she tried to funnel his determination. Richard Hanson believed a person could do anything if their commitment to the task was strong enough. *If you can't fly, then run. If you can't run, then walk. If you can't walk, then crawl. But whatever you do, you have to keep moving forward.* It was something she'd heard her father recite many times, a quote by Martin Luther King, Jr.

"You shouldn't have come," the man said when she finally reached him, his face pale, his eyes wide. "My leg is pinned. You need to go back."

"Too late!" she yelled above the

roar of the wind. *Stay with me, Lord.* She stuck her head underneath the water, but it was thick as Texas fog, and she couldn't see anything. When she lifted her head, the sting of mascara in her eyes distracted her for a few moments as she blinked and dabbed at her eyes with her wet ZZ Top T-shirt. She jumped when she felt something brush against her foot, an unidentifiable object that stung as it passed by her. A branch, maybe. It felt like a deep paper cut. "I called 9-1-1, but who knows how long it will take for them to get here, or if they can even get through. We need to get you to my car somehow."

He shook his head. "I can't get

my leg free. The higher the water got, the harder I've tried."

Alex glanced around as the skies spit a light trickle of rain, but the wind was like a dozen tornadoes funneling around them. As two large branches drifted by, she silently asked God for help again.

"Do you have any idea what has you pinned? A branch or something?" She ran her fingers underneath her eyes, hoping to clear the blackness she was sure the mascara had left. It seemed an odd time to notice the man's square jaw, intense blue eyes, and a dimple on one side only. She wondered what the rest of him looked like beneath the water. Was he tall? He was crouched in the water, so it was hard to tell.

If she didn't clear her mind, he was going to drown.

"I don't know. I thought it was a branch, but I'm not really sure." His voice was gargled, like maybe he'd already swallowed water, and there was an urgency in his tone that caused a jolt of adrenaline to rush through Alex's veins and slam against her chest.

"I'm guessing you are in a lot of pain?" She flinched when he did.

He latched onto her arm. "Listen . . ." He spoke loudly, against the roar of the wind. "You must get back to your car and get out of here. Go now, while you can. I'm sure someone will show up soon, and they'll have equipment to get me out."

Alex eyed the water that was now up to his bottom lip as she stood towering above him. Swallowing hard, she took a deep breath. If she left him, she'd see his face in her dreams — nightmares — for the rest of her life. "I'm not leaving you here. What's your name?" He was breathing faster as he struggled to hold his head higher.

"Parker. Listen . . ." he said again, breathing hard. "I have a son, Spencer. Please find him, and you tell him that Daddy went to be with Mommy, and tell him . . . tell him I love him with everything I am, and —"

"Stop! You're not going to die. I'll get you out of here." Alex heard the shakiness in her voice. In the corner of her eyes she saw the street lights go out, along with the festive strings of Christmas lights connecting them. The wreaths dangling from the middle of the display shone brightly, which seemed odd to Alex.

Parker shook his head. “No. I’m stuck.” He was still clutching her arm. “Please promise me that you’ll find my son. His aunt got him safely off the island earlier today, but when it’s safe, please find him, tell him . . .” His voice trailed off as he let go of her arm. A wave slammed into his face, filling his mouth with water, and the more he sputtered, the more he choked. He was breathing way too hard. Alex hadn’t had more than basic first-aid classes, but she could tell he was panicking.

"How old is Spencer?" She bent at the waist and put her face closer to his until he finally locked eyes with her, a rhythmic set of mini rapids swooshing between and around them.

"Four," he said barely loud enough for Alex to hear as he lifted his chin higher. "Dear, God . . ." he whispered, closing his eyes. His hand found Alex's and he squeezed. "Will you pray with me?"

Alex had been praying since she took her first step into the rushing river of saltwater that was rising. "Yes," she said as she cupped his cheek with her other hand. "Dear Lord, please give us the courage and strength to free Parker from whatever is holding him in the water. Please, God . . ."

"No . . . I need to . . ." More water found its way into Parker's mouth, followed by more choking. Alex waited while he caught his breath again. "I — I ask you God to forgive my trespasses, my sins . . ."

Alex scanned the area as best she could. Not a soul in sight. Floodwater had risen halfway up the tires of her Honda. She was wise enough to know that if Parker went completely underwater, he would likely grab onto her in a panic, possibly taking her underwater also. She'd no sooner had the thought when the rains began to subside. There was still a fierce wind, but maybe they were buying some time. *Thank you, God.* She also thought she heard a siren in the distance.

"Tell me your name," Parker said as his teeth chattered. It wasn't cold, so she wasn't sure what was happening. These first couple of weeks in November had been unseasonably warm.

"Alex. Short for Alexandria."

The hint of a smile played across his lips. "You're a brave woman, Alexandria."

"No one calls me that, except for my father." She thought again about the man she loved most in the world. "And I'm not really brave, but I'm not leaving you."

Parker held her gaze. "Yes, you

will. And you *should.* You should go now."

Alex shook her head. "No. We aren't giving up. Help is on the way."

Parker smiled a little again. "If you can't fly, then run. If you can't run, then walk. If you can't walk, then crawl. But whatever you do, you have to keep moving forward."

Alex froze, stopped breathing for a few seconds. "Martin Luther King, Jr."

"Yes." He let out a long, controlled sigh. "A good man."

Alex's eyes filled with tears. There was no doubt in her mind that her father had died. She didn't know how she knew, but she did. *He was another good man.*

"What's wrong?" Parker waved an arm atop the rapids around them. "Besides the obvious?"

"My father just died." She wasn't sure why she blurted it out to a stranger, but she was confident in her statement, and within seconds, she was crying.

Parker's fingers brushed against hers beneath the water and found her palm, intertwining his fingers with hers. "I'm so sorry. When? Recently?"

Just now. She couldn't tell him that. "Yes."

He squeezed her hand. "Alexandria, I am very sorry for your loss."

"Thank you."

They were quiet for a few moments, and there was actually a trickle of sunlight peeking through the clouds.

"The eye of the storm," Parker said, a tinge of hope in his voice. "It's not even that big of a hurricane."

Alex swiped at her eyes, drawing back black fingertips. "Mascara. I probably look like a raccoon."

Parker was still holding her hand. "You are the most beautiful raccoon I've ever seen."

"Oh, I'm sure I am," she said, trying to smile, needing to lighten the fear and strengthen her resolve.

Alex had noticed how handsome he was earlier. She'd learned a long time ago to never get too attracted to someone who was sitting down, or in Parker's case — hunched over in dangerous floodwaters. Alex was five-foot-ten. She recalled meeting Jimmy Strasburg on a blind date in college. He had arrived at the agreed upon meeting place before she did, and he was already seated. They talked for two hours, got along wonderfully. Then Jimmy stood up. He couldn't have been an inch over five-foot-two, and with her heels on, Alex had towered over him like an island palm tree when they'd left the restaurant. It was silly. Height certainly shouldn't define a person, but she supposed everyone had dating requirements. Five-ten or taller was one of hers.

A gust of wind sent a rushing surge of water over Parker's face, and when his face was visible again, his wide eyes revealed his panic as he coughed water, straining to raise his chin higher. It started to rain again, and Alex's stomach lurched. But she needed him still and calm.

"Do you have plans for the holidays? Thanksgiving isn't far away." She hoped her voice sounded steadier than it felt.

"I know you're trying to make small talk so I won't panic." He took in a gulp of air before water splashed across his face again.

Alex winced as he squeezed her hand underwater. "Is it working?"

His expression stilled. "What are the chances that I would be here, in this predicament, with you, and that you'll be the last person I'll see on this earth?"

"Do. Not. Give. Up." She turned in every direction, but didn't see anyone, and the siren she'd thought she heard earlier was either gone or she'd imagined it. "Help is coming."

"My son lost his mother, and it seems unfair that he's going to lose me, too, without getting to know either one of us very well."

Parker seemed to be settling in on the fact that he was going to die. Only once had Alex ever faced death head on. She'd had a severe reaction to an antibiotic that had left her covered from head to toe with a nasty rash that would eventually take months to recover from. But it was the threat of Stevens-

Johnson syndrome that had terrified her at the time. She could still recall the look on the doctor's face when she'd asked, "Can this kill me?" The female dermatologist had nodded. Up until that point, she'd always thought her faith was solid, but when faced with her own demise, she'd been terrified. The way Parker was now.

The rain pounded them now with a relentless vengeance, large pellets battering and bouncing off their heads like dull needles against a pincushion. Waves were pushing forward with a force that could only come with a rising tide, and as Alex saw a large sheet of plywood float by in the water, she wondered how much more dangerous and heavy debris was floating by beneath the surface of the tenebrous waters.

"You're not going to die," she said with as much conviction as she could, but as the water rose higher and higher, Parker could barely fend off the swells pushing into his mouth. *Please, God.*

Parker stared into Alex's eyes, longing to see his soul in the reflection, wondering if it would be an easy trip to the other side, and praying he would be going in the right direction. He'd heard stories about people seeing loved ones right before they passed to the next life, whispering their names as they drifted over. He searched this woman's eyes again, looking for Cecelia, but all he saw was the terror in Alex's eyes. He owed this stranger more than he'd ever be able to give her.

"The moment my nose and mouth are underwater, turn and look away. Go quickly . . ." He paused, holding his mouth closed as a wave of water lapped all the way to his forehead before receding. "Go quickly to your car. Don't let my drowning be the very last thing you see." He paused again. "You really should go now."

She shook her head. "No. Help will come."

Bless her for staying, but . . . "Do you have children?" He spoke louder than before so she could hear him above the fierce winds encircling them.

"Nope. Not married, no children. I haven't found the right man yet."

"I find that hard to believe."

She smiled a little. "True story." Her bottom lip trembled as she squeezed his hand.

"What will you do for the holidays?" It was small talk, but Parker's heart was beating way too fast, and if he didn't drown soon, he feared he would have a heart attack. Maybe that would be the lesser of the two evils he faced. A few hours ago, Christmas lights had flickered on the Strand, even though merchants were busy boarding up their windows. Now everything had gone dark. Even the

Christmas wreaths that had stayed lit longer than anything else.

"I don't know."

He didn't say anything, took a deep breath, and waited as the water rose above his mouth. He tried to wiggle free of Alex's hold on his hand, but she just clung tighter. He didn't know it was possible to breathe so fast through his nose, and he waited for Cecelia to make herself known. But once again, the water receded to his chin as the wind stilled, which would only be temporary, until the next surge. Parker figured he wouldn't outlast more than a couple more waves.

"It's just been me and my dad for a long time," Alex said. "My mom died when I was young. We spent nearly every holiday at the beach, and always on Christmas day." She was almost screaming now since the winds had picked up, and probably because she was scared. "My house is on Crystal Beach, a little east of Galveston on the Bolivar Peninsula. My dad helped me get it after Hurricane Ike hit in 2008 and we got a really great deal. Everything was kind of a mess for a while, but we both knew it was the only way I'd ever be able to afford a house right on the beach." She shrugged, shaking. "Anyway, we always set up a small table by the sea and ate fish tacos. It might sound silly to some people, but it was our thing. We even wore goofy

Christmas hats." Black streaks of mascara trailed down her cheeks. She recalled her father always calling their holiday Christmas by the Sea. "My dad always wanted to be a boat captain, but he worked as a carpenter instead, giving up his own dreams so I would have a normal and happy life." She paused, recalling her idyllic childhood, wondering how she was going to live without her father. Hopefully, her parents were dancing in heaven and would be sharing fish tacos on Christmas day. "It will be my first time to eat tacos on Christmas day by myself."

"I'm sorry about your father." Parker wasn't sure he'd ever felt a connection to another human being the way he did to this woman now. Except maybe his son. And Cecelia. Maybe it was because he was going to die holding her hand. He knew she wouldn't leave until he'd gone still in the water. Even though she should.

Dirty water rushed by them carrying everything from dead fish to floating bags of trash. Two large branches swam atop the rapids, followed by a Burger King bag, an empty toilet paper roll, and a couple of empty cups with straws protruding from the lids. The pain in his leg had subsided to a dull ache, but his chest had tightened to the point he almost couldn't breathe. Then it happened.

A big rush of water.

He clamped his mouth closed, but when it receded, it only receded to just below his nostrils. The next surge would be it. Alex was crying as she held his hand, but then she jerked away from him, turned, and started struggling against the current to get to her car. He couldn't say a word because she was doing exactly what he'd told her to do. But if he'd been able to talk, he would have begged her to stay. He closed his eyes and prayed.

Seconds later, her hand was on his arm, and she was holding a paper cup that had floated by. One ear remained barely above the water, and Parker heard sirens. Or was he imagining it? Glancing to his left, he thought he'd seen movement. *Cecelia?* He thought he heard Christmas music.

"I know you can hear me, but can't speak, so listen." Alex spoke firmly, as if this was the most important thing she was ever going to say in her life. "Your nose is going to go underwater soon, but you can breath through this straw as long as the other end stays above the water. I hear sirens. Help is close. So, don't panic." She lowered the straw into the water, her finger plugging the end that Parker eased into his mouth, wrapping his lips around it and her finger before she slowly took her hand away. He filled his lungs with a long breath of air, trying hard not to panic.

Parker heard the sirens. *They're*

coming. He did his best to force himself calm, and just as she'd said, the water rose above his nose. Clamping his nostrils closed with one hand, he clung to her other hand as he breathed through the straw. Too big of a wave would cause him to intake water, panic, and she'd never get the straw back in his mouth. It seemed odd that he would have such a rational thought, but as Spencer's face flashed in his mind's eye, he prayed for God to keep his breathing steady.

As the tide that engulfed them continued to rise, only a couple of inches of the straw cleared the water. His new friend was going to lose this heroic battle.

When the straw slipped from his mouth, he held his breath, but it was only seconds before he gagged and water began to fill his lungs. The space around him went black, and finally . . . there was Cecelia. Smiling. Floating nearby. Her arms open. But Spencer's face bounced around his mind, the reminder of all that he was leaving behind. Parker felt like he was crying, but it was hard to tell. His body was going limp. Total darkness. *Where is the light? Why is there no light? Where did Cecelia go? Where is Alex?* She'd seen him die, or so she thought, so she'd fled. *Good.* Maybe she'd left before all the thrashing started. *Did I thrash?* He wasn't sure.

Then a surge of horrific pain engulfed his lower leg, and he was sure his foot was being sawed off with a dull, serrated knife. But he was too tired to struggle. *Too dead,* he assumed.

Alex cringed as she ducked below the dirty water and wrapped both arms around Parker's legs, pulling with all her might as blood circled and swooshed around them like the scene of a shark attack. She eventually tugged hard enough to get him loose and was able to get his head above water, but his body was limp, heavy like dead weight. *Is he dead?*

As she struggled to hold onto him from behind and keep his head above water, she repeatedly lost her footing, twice almost losing them both to the wrath of the current. The sirens were getting closer, but she wasn't sure she could hold him for much longer. Ferocious winds churned the fast-moving water into a sea of rapids carrying even more debris. Tears, mixed with mascara and saltwater, burned her eyes as long strands of hair whipped across her face in every direction. *Please God, help me to hold onto him.* When her legs began to tremble, she didn't think she had enough energy left to fight the current, and there was a burning sensation below her knee, along with eddies of blood. *His or hers,* she wondered?

In the distance, her Honda Civic was giving up the fight. Alex's heart pounded against the wall of her chest as the water lifted the car from the elevated spot where she'd parked, carrying it away — along with whatever hope she had left. But then she saw headlights, and with a burst of superpower, she tightened her grip on Parker and fought shaky legs as tears drizzled down her cheeks. Two men emerged from a pickup truck, and not far behind there was an ambulance.

"Stay where you are!" One of the men secured a belt of some type around his waist, while the other one hooked the other end to the bumper of the truck. The vehicle was much further away than where Alex had left her car; that entire area was submerged now.

The man covered the distance between the truck and Alex in less than a minute, but with slow and steady steps as the water rushed around him.

"It's him. He's the one really hurt." Alex heard the shakiness in her voice and felt the rattle in her throat, but when the rescuer took over, she fought not to melt into the current.

A few minutes later, they were on high ground, and two paramedics took over, administering CPR to Parker while the original two guys, presumably volunteers, cleaned up the cut on Alex's leg. But she never took her eyes off of Parker, praying that he'd wake up.

Finally, he sputtered water, but when he became fully conscious, his blood pressure was so high, the paramedics called the hospital, asking permission to give Parker something to ease the pain. Within a few minutes, he was comfortably sleeping in the back of the ambulance. The rain had slowed, as if God had a protective umbrella over them.

"Can I ride in the ambulance with him?" Alex touched his foot, the one that wasn't injured and the only part of his body she could reach from where she was standing.

"We don't have room. There's another emergency up the road." One of the breathless paramedics climbed inside the ambulance and sat next to Parker. “We need the room, but if you’re his wife . . . can you follow us?”

Alex shook her head. “I’m not his wife, but my car washed away while all of this was going on, and —”

“We can give you a ride to wherever you need to go.” It was the man who had braved the current to rescue Alex and Parker.

She glanced back and forth between the paramedic still standing at the back of the ambulance and the man who had saved hers and Parker’s lives. “Can we follow the ambulance to the hospital?”

“Sure.”

Alex took another long look at Parker before the doors closed. “Is he going to be okay?”

The paramedic nodded. “Yeah, I believe so. His foot is in pretty bad shape, but all of his vitals are stable. His blood pressure was probably high from the pain, but I think he will be all right.”

Alex took a long cleansing breath, then walked with the two volunteers to their truck. Water was already inching up the tires. They’d barely cleared the hazardous area when one of them took a phone call, and it was easy enough for Alex to tell from one side of the conversation that they weren’t going to the hospital.

The passenger in the front seat looked over his shoulder at Alex. “I’m sorry Ma’am, we’ve got another emergency, so we can’t follow the ambulance to Houston right now."

Alex nodded. "I understand. I have a friend who lives nearby if you want to drop me there, or I'll ride with you to wherever you need to go." She shivered at the thought of being at any other accident scene. But the passenger made a quick phone call, then turned back to Alex. "Where does your friend live?"

After she'd explained, the man nodded and turned to the driver. "We should be able to avoid heavy flooding to get her to friend's place. Jim and Marty are almost to the other emergency. Let's drop her at her friend's house."

"Thank you," she said barely

above a whisper, but then she cleared her throat. “Do you know what that man’s last name was, the one they took away in the ambulance?”

One man shook his head while the other said, “No. I didn’t even hear his first name.”

Alex wished she’d asked Parker his last name, but she assumed they were taking him to a Houston hospital further inland. She’d find him later. Right now, she had another call to make.

“I hate to even ask this but . . . my father is in John Sealy Hospital, and I urgently need to call him. Would it be possible to borrow a cell phone?” Alex’s purse and belongings had been submerged in her car. Sniffling, she couldn't stop trembling, despite the blanket she'd been given after being pulled from the rushing water.

"Sure." The passenger reached over the seat and handed her his phone. They were both young guys, maybe late twenties, around Alex's age. "Call as many people as you need to. You've been through quite an ordeal. But click over if another call comes in." He smiled. "You saved that guy's life."

While my father was dying less than a mile away. She Googled John Sealy Hospital, and a few minutes later, she heard a familiar voice.

"Alex, we've been trying to reach you." Nurse Karen's soft whisper confirmed what Alex already knew to be true.

Moments later, she handed the guy his phone, crying hard now.

"Wow, I'm real sorry for your loss," the driver said, not going more than ten miles an hour, the car swaying in the wind as he did his best through high water. "You've already been through a lot today."

Alex pulled the blanket snug around her, and it wasn't long before her quiet sobs turned to uncontrollable crying. *I'm sorry I wasn't there, Daddy.*

Parker swam in and out of consciousness, aware that he was in an ambulance, and later knowing he was in a hospital. His eyes were closed, but the smell of ammonia and beeping machines alerted him as to where he was. Maybe he wasn't going to die after all.

As he stared at the back of his eyelids, it wasn't Cecelia he saw, but the vision of an angel who had rescued him. Her long dark hair swooped in wild strands across her face, black mascara trailing down her cheeks, the fear in her eyes. *Alex.*

He was slipping away again. *Tired. Sleep.*

When he woke up, there were three doctors standing at the foot of the bed, along with his sister — and Spencer. *Thank you, God.* His four-year-old son stood next to Angie, Parker's only sibling.

"Hey, Buddy." Parker held his arm out to his son, who rushed to him, burying his head in the nook of Parker's shoulder. "Daddy's okay," he said in a shaky whisper. He swallowed back the knot in his throat as he clung to his son's love like a life raft. "I'm okay," he repeated softly, as much for himself as for Spencer.

But am I okay? Something felt amiss below his left knee, hollow.

Angie came around the other side, leaned down, and kissed Parker on the cheek. "Welcome back. You've been sleeping for two days."

"Where . . . ?" He scanned the room. Three male doctors who didn't look any older than Parker stood quietly. "Where is the woman, the one who helped me?"

"I don't know anything about her," the shortest of the young doctors said, as if Alex was just a random person of no consequence. "But we do need to talk to you, Mr. McIntyre." The guy — Dr. Easton, his badge read — glanced at Angie, who quickly went to the other side of the bed.

"Hey, Spence," she said softly. "Let's take a walk while the doctors talk to Daddy."

His son clung tightly to Parker's arm, but eventually let Angie take him out of the room.

This is bad. He waited, searching each of the three men's faces for a clue. The short doctor cleared his throat. He seemed to be the one in control. The boss.

"You're going to be fine, Parker, but the damage to your foot was extensive, and we were unable to repair the cartilage. I'm afraid we had to perform an amputation a few inches below your knee. But the good news is that you are a strong candidate for a prosthetic device once the area has healed."

Parker's heart thumped against his chest in a way that caused his vision to blur. The next thing he knew, a nurse was in the room putting a shot of something in his IV, nothing strong enough to keep him from throwing back the covers on his bed. He couldn't remember the last time he'd cried prior to the accident, but now he bawled like a baby. There was a huge white bandage, a stump. *I don't have a foot.*

Darkness again. *Did someone turn out the light? Or am I seeing the back of my eyelids?*

His heart stopped pounding, the heaviness lifted.

Alex spent two days on her friend's couch in Galveston. Gina's apartment building had stayed high and dry, despite the continued rains and flooding. Alex focused on finding Parker. She'd used Gina's phone to check hospitals, but she hadn't been able to find him. *Difficult without a last name.*

When some of the roads cleared, Alex's best friend, Shelley, picked her up and took her back to her apartment in Houston since there wasn't a clear route to Alex's house yet. They stopped at Walmart on the way to pick up a cheap cell phone since Alex's had been lost when her car was washed away. Alex continued her search for Parker with no luck. She'd called every hospital on the outskirts of Galveston, most of them full and overflowing with patients who had been relocated prior to the storm. Her father had been deemed too critical to move, and he'd been taken to the safest wing of the hospital during the storm. *Only to die anyway.*

"Still no word on the guy?" Shelley Armstrong sipped on a Red Bull next to Alex on the couch, her bare feet on the coffee table while videos of the aftermath of the storm scrolled across the television. Most of the water had receded, but the devastation was massive.

Alex and Shelley had grown up together, but Shelley had made the move to Houston when she landed a job working as a paralegal for a law firm. Alex had been fortunate to find work on the island as a human resources manager for a large hotel chain.

"No. I still haven't been able to find him." Alex was desperate to learn what happened to Parker, and she'd chastised herself repeatedly for not getting his last name. She had watched the news on television since she'd been staying at Shelley's, hoping for a glimpse of her car, a mention about Parker, or anything that might help her to locate him. But nothing. No one was being let back onto the island, and Alex's father was in the morgue at John Sealy Hospital. She'd been crying on and off since she'd arrived at Shelley's apartment.

"When things calm down, I bet you'll be able to find him." Shelley put a hand on Alex's leg and patted her twice, as if everything would be okay. Alex wasn't sure things would ever be alright. She had nightmares. Parker's wild eyes when he went underwater. Her Herculean strength as she tore his leg from whatever held it beneath the water. Keeping him upright in a current that should have swept them both away. The medical personnel intercepting him, pushing Alex out of the way. Her not being able to ride in the ambulance.

She picked up her cell phone. She had eight more hospitals to try, even though she'd already called the closest ones to Galveston, and now she was trying hospitals way on the other side of Houston. Seven calls later, and still no luck. But she dialed the number for the eighth one on the list. *Please God, I've got to find him.*

Two weeks later, Parker was released from the hospital, even though there would be all kinds of follow-up appointments and rehab. Angie packed his things as he stared at the wheelchair by the bed. Eventually, he would advance to crutches, and then if all went well, he'd be fitted for a prosthetic leg.

"The guy I talked to at your office — Jake — said there isn't a rush to get back to work," Angie said. "He said to take your time."

Parker nodded. He'd talked to Jake during his hospital stay, but for some reason, the phone in his room wasn't working today, and he wasn't getting good cell service either. "Thanks for calling him. Where's Spencer?" Parker sat up in bed and slung his legs over the side. His one-and-a-half legs.

"Maryanne, a nurse where I work

has two children close to Spencer's age, and she's off today. Great people. I thought it might be good for Spencer to have some playtime while we get you settled at the condo, then I'll pick him up."

Parker's temporary home would be a condo in Houston. He disliked Houston. Too busy. He couldn't smell the ocean, watch the boats come in, or walk the beach. Although he wouldn't be walking anywhere soon.

He wondered how long it would be before he'd be back in his house. Mostly he wondered why he hadn't been able to find a woman named Alexandria who lived at Crystal Beach. He was angry with himself for not getting her last name. And to his recollection, he hadn't given her his full name either.

As he thought about Spencer, he knew that he would forever be in debt to a woman named Alex who had made sure he lived, at great personal risk to herself. Her face was etched into his brain forever. The fear. The determination. The . . . beauty.

They had prayed together, and he'd been sure her face would be the last one he'd see in this life. But now, he couldn't find her, and doing so was a top priority.

"Did you tell Jake about the two files in my desk drawer?" Parker stared at the white lump of bandages a few inches below his knee. It didn't hurt anymore. It was just a void. *I don't have a foot anymore.* But he'd tried to keep his life organized as best he could from the hospital, and making sure his boss had two client files was a part of that effort.

"Yeah, I did." Angie zipped a small, red suitcase she'd brought him early on. A few clothes, socks, toothbrush, and a Bible. Two hospital chaplains had been by twice each, to talk to Parker about how blessed he was, citing those who had lost their lives in the storm. Parker didn't need convincing. He knew he was blessed. He'd lost his foot, and that was something that didn't come easily. He'd gone through the expected range of emotions, from sadness to anger to acceptance. But he was alive. And he was going to see his son grow into a man, good Lord willing.

"Are you sure you don't want me to stay with you a while at the rental?" Angie sighed as she set the packed suitcase by the door.

"No. I'll be able to drive soon. My condo is on the first floor. And I know you're a phone call away."

"You can't drive *yet.*" Angie's voice had a firm, but gentle, tone to it. She reminded him of their mother when she talked like she was now.

Their parents were on an extended vacation, or an early retirement. Parker and Angie weren't sure, but at the moment, Mom and Dad were with a tour group in

Spain, not expected to be home until after the holidays. Parker had to talk his mother out of getting on the next plane home. His parents had saved money and made plans to spend this year traveling, and Parker had repeatedly explained to his mom that Angie had things under control, that they should carry on with their vacation. They could continue to Skype, and Parker promised to keep his parents updated on his progress, assuring them that he was okay and would learn to function without the lower part of one leg. *Eventually.*

He'd mostly moved past the angry phase, but those emotions still reared up occasionally. When they did, it was Parker's first instinct to lash out at God. Instead, he forced himself to stow any rage and to thank the Lord for sparing his life. Spencer was an easy reminder that Parker needed to be grateful.

Poor Spencer would probably never get to do anything exciting in his entire life, since Parker was already overprotective. Losing Cecelia had left Parker feeling like he'd never survive if something happened to Spencer. When he thought about how close he'd come to leaving his son without any parents at all, his thoughts drifted to the woman who had saved his life.

Alex. Where was she?

Alex lay two red roses on her father's grave. The headstone still hadn't arrived, but it had only been a couple of weeks since she'd ordered it. She'd come to visit him every day since the funeral, and now with Thanksgiving only a few days away, she still cried every time she visited. She'd still been searching for Parker, but twenty-three hospitals later, she still had no information. Maybe she was just never meant to know him. She was there, at the right time, at the right moment. *Fate? God's will that they met, never to see each other again?* With each day, she was accepting that reality, although she'd see his eyes, the look before he completely went underwater, for the rest of her life. But she could recall his square jaw and his handsome features too. She wanted to remember him forever, and she was sure she would.

"I'm off to work, Daddy." Alex kissed her fingertips, then pressed them against the dirt of her father's grave, the mound slowly flattening with each of her visits.

Taking a deep breath, she got in her rental car, an ugly dark green Camry that her insurance company provided. She'd gotten a new drivers license, Social Security card, and replaced other items she'd lost during the flood. The loss of life had hit a hundred, and there were still dozens in Galveston hospitals and other facilities in Houston. Most of those killed were the ones who hadn't left the island, the old timers who had survived many a hurricane, some as far back as Hurricanes Alicia and Carmen. Both before Alex's time.

She'd just started driving toward the cemetery exit when she heard music coming from her purse. She put her foot on the brake and dug around inside her bag until she found the phone and answered.

"You're still coming for Thanksgiving, right?" Shelley was hosting her entire family in her small apartment for the holiday. Alex wasn't sure how she'd fit even one more person. Shelley said she was expecting eighteen.

"Yeah, I'll be there. Thanks, Shelley."

Alex would have preferred to sit

on the beach and eat tacos with her father, watch the boats, the waves, and inhale the briny smells of an ocean they both loved, but that wasn't going to happen this year. Shelley had been insistent that Alex spend the holiday with her and her family, and maybe it was best Alex not be alone on this first holiday without her beloved father.

Hopefully, her father had found her mother and they were both gazing upon a great ocean in heaven, eating all the fish tacos that they could consume.

And hopefully Alex would start to feel normal again some day.

It was the first week of December when Parker walked across his living room, receiving applause from his son and Angie. The prosthetic half-leg was temporary, but it gave him mobility he hadn't had until now, and he was thankful. Eventually, he'd have a custom fit prosthesis. He was also grateful that Angie had put up a Christmas tree in his condo, decorated it, and filled it with gifts underneath. Angie didn't have a lot of money. Nurses were extremely underpaid. He realized that even more after his accident. But Angie packed every single thing individually, even if it was something small from the Dollar Store. She'd wrap it in a big box, and every year, the amount of presents under the tree grew, giving them an exaggerated vision of the amount of money she spent on gifts. But the focus had always been on family and blessings, something beautiful that their parents had passed down during their modest childhoods. Parker was glad his folks had been able to save some money over the years, enough to travel the way they'd always planned.

"Are we going to go see Santa today?" Spencer's toothy smile stretched across his precious face, his bright blue eyes anxious to experience the season. This year more than ever, Parker was excited to watch his son open presents.

"Um, I need to ask you something." Angie took a deep breath and blew it out slowly.

What now? She'd already helped him battle it out with the health insurance company about services that providers had deemed unnecessary. She'd also been the one to inform him that his deductible was five thousand dollars. Parker couldn't recall being sick prior to this, so he hadn't ever looked closely at his policy, which was proving to be a nightmare. But when his sister smiled, he thought he caught a twinkle in her eyes. "What?" he finally asked.

"I know we said we were going to have a quiet Christmas together, just you, me, and Spencer at my apartment, since Mom and Dad are traveling, but . . ." Yep, there was a twinkle in his sister's eyes.

"Do you mind if someone else joins us?" She folded her hands in front of her, another gesture that reminded Parker of their mother. "His name is Joe."

Parker grinned. *"Joe?"*

Angie nodded, smiling. His sister had been married before, for a total of six months. Parker recalled wanting to beat the guy to a pulp for cheating on Angie, taking the little bit of money she'd saved, and filing for divorce. But Angie had been the stronger one when they were growing up, and she still was, even during her own divorce.

"Of course, *Joe* can come." Parker wanted his sister happy, and if Joe would brighten her holidays, Parker was all for it.

Angie sat down on the couch next to him. "Joe's great, Parker." Grinning like a schoolgirl, she added, "Handsome . . . and he's a doctor."

"Really?" Parker's smile grew. "Not too surprising, I guess, since you're a nurse."

She cleared her throat as she sat taller on the couch twisting to face him. "Actually, he was one of *your* doctors when you were in the hospital. I didn't meet him at the hospital where I work."

"Oh." Parker raised an eyebrow. "Which one?"

Angie smiled. "He was with the group of doctors who first told you that they'd had to amputate your foot."

"The short guy or one of the

other ones?"

"He isn't that short." Angie grimaced a little, but it didn't last long. His sister wasn't all that tall anyway, and she was giddy and glowing again within a few seconds.

"Of course you can invite your new doctor boyfriend for Christmas." He leaned back against the couch and propped his fake leg up on the coffee table. Angie had told him repeatedly not to call it a fake leg, so the phrase was something Parker had taken up only in his mind.

She locked eyes with him, smiling. "Thanks, Parker." She gave him a hug, then stood up. "I'm going to go." She went to Spencer, kissed and hugged him, then headed to the door, turning to face him before she left. "I know you'll find someone special too."

Parker smiled. He already had. He just couldn't locate her.

Alex carried two folding chairs from her house to the beach. She'd tried to ignore the holiday all together, but by the end of the day, she was resolved to revisit her family tradition, if only to carry it on for a final time. She set up the chairs, then went back to the house to retrieve the small table that she'd been putting between the reclining seats for years. In Texas, Christmas was either shorts and T-shirts or down jackets. The temperature varied year to year, ranging within thirty degrees. This year, it was somewhere in between. Not cold enough for a jacket, but not warm enough for shorts. Jeans and a short-sleeve shirt, with a light jacket nearby.

She opened the bag of fish tacos, the ones from a small shack up the road. The place wasn't open on Christmas Day, but Alex always picked up the tacos the day before for her and her father. Biting into one of the tacos, she stared out at the sea as the sun began its descent. Two boats were in the far distance, the waves were calm, and all of the beach debris from the storm had been cleared. She'd only had minor damage to her house and was able to get back in it a few days after the storm, but some homes — those not high enough and sturdy enough — were still undergoing repairs. But not today. Not on Christmas.

She closed her eyes, savoring the taste of the scrumptious taco as the light breeze carried the smell of the ocean, wafting up her nostrils like a familiar friend. She'd visited her father's grave earlier in the day, but otherwise chosen to stay home, despite Shelley's attempts to get her out of the house on Christmas. But the day had been filled with Christmas movies on TV, memories of her father, and now — the greatest fish tacos on earth.

"I miss you, Dad." She held up a champagne glass filled with sparkling grape cider. "Merry Christmas."

The beach was quiet, one of the best things about having Christmas tacos on the beach on Christmas Day. She picked up her Christmas hat, glancing at the one in the empty chair next to her. It was silly and wonderful. Alex had bought the hats during a time when her father was having chemo and had lost his hair. They'd had so much fun wearing them, that they'd worn them every year since. Alex figured she'd retire them after this year, stash the hats in her mother's cedar chest. But as a tribute to her father, she sat on the beach eating tacos and wearing her Santa hat. She set the other hat in the chair next to her. But a movement down the beach caught her eye.

"Ugh," she said through a mouthful. It was a guy. He was by himself. And he was likely going to want to make small talk, or tell her some horrific story about why he was by himself on Christmas. All of which would mess up the little bit of the day she had left. Behind him, there was another couple and a child.

She picked up an emergency book she'd brought, a habit she'd long ago adopted, even when it wasn't Christmas and she just wanted to be alone on the beach. Burying her head in it, she could feel him approaching, but she didn't look up. Until he stopped right in front of her.

“Hello, Merry Christmas,” she said with a mouthful of taco, her head still in the book. Hopefully, he’d get the hint and just walk away.

“Merry Christmas.”

Alex’s eyes slowly lifted, her mouth stuffed with food. Her heart skipped a beat as she locked eyes with a familiar face. She dropped her taco in the sand as she slowly stood up.

“It’s you,” she said as she struggled to swallow what was in her mouth, her knees weak, her heart thudding in her chest. “It’s you,” she repeated as she walked closer to him and smiled. “I looked for you.” The words barely whispered across her lips as her eyes filled with tears. "I looked for you," she said again softly.

"I was here Thanksgiving, but I couldn't walk very well at the time, and I couldn't find you. You said you and your father had shared holidays on the beach, so I took a chance." He shrugged a little, grinning. "And I took another chance today, which certainly paid off. I've been looking for you too."

Alex stood up, knowing she must look a wreck and probably had taco sauce on her chin. She gave it a quick swipe, but she couldn't stop smiling. "You're tall."

Parker chuckled. "Yeah, since I was about fourteen."

"Are you . . . did you . . . recover okay?" She looked Parker up and down. He was in jeans and a white T-shirt, wearing tennis shoes.

"Sort of." He lifted his left pant leg, revealing a leg that wasn't the one he was born with.

"Oh no." Alex covered her face with her hands as she shook her head. "I'm so sorry. I'm so very sorry. I — I . . ."

Strong hands landed on top of hers. He eased them away from her face as they stood facing each other. "How could you be sorry? You saved my life."

"But your foot." She looked down again, his pant leg now covering the prosthetic. "It's gone."

"Yep. Gone." He grinned. "It was just a foot."

She appreciated that he was trying to make light of it, but it had to have been devastating. Rarely speechless, Alex stared into his crystal blue eyes.

He brushed back strands of her hair that had swept across her face, then straightened her Santa hat, smiling. "I almost didn't recognize you without raccoon eyes." Inching closer, he said, "Nothing would have ever been right in my universe if I hadn't been able to find you, to thank you for saving my life."

A tear trickled down Alex's cheek, and she didn't bother to swipe it away. She'd never given up seeing Parker again, but a surreal feeling swept over her as he stepped even closer. She leaned up, breathing in his musky scent and the smell of something minty on his breath. But instead of kissing her, he put his arms around her and pulled her head to his broad chest, hugging her tightly. “It’s you,” he said in a whisper.

“It’s you,” she repeated easing away from him to look him in the eyes again, to make sure she wasn’t dreaming. Then she reached down and picked up her father’s Santa hat and handed it to him.

“Are you sure? I know it was your dad’s.” He paused. “A special time for the two of you.”

She nodded, smiling, feeling the same bond she’d felt with him in the water. He leaned down, and she put the hat on him. “You look great,” she said, sniffling.

"So do you," he said as he adjusted the hat on his head. "Now." He smiled. "I'd like to know if you'd like to go out with me? On a date."

Alex couldn't wipe the grin from her face as the wind swirled around them in a cool and comforting way, as if repaying them for the hurricane. Bursts of sunlight met with the horizon in a postcard vision of possibilities for the future. "I would like that."

He cupped her chin. "I should probably warn you. I'm not going to wait until a formal goodbye after a date to kiss you. It's going to happen right now."

Alex swallowed hard. "I'm not strong enough to fight you off," she said, grinning.

"Oh, I'm fairly sure you could run away without me being able to catch you." He glanced down at his leg, grinning.

Alex didn't wait for him to make the move. She leaned up and kissed him with everything she had, totally prepared for the entire past event to flash before her in nightmarish visions. But instead, God gifted her with something else. A flash of a future that she could have with this man. They kissed again, then she eased away, staring into his eyes again before they turned to face the ocean, his arm protectively around her. Movement to their right caused them to shift their stance. A small boy was skipping toward them ahead of two adults, his blond hair blowing in the wind as he playfully slowed his stride to kick the sand, leaning down to pick up an occasional shell.

"Awe, he's cute." Alex let her eyes soak in the innocence of youth, carefree and happy. Then she turned back to Parker, silently thanking God for this magical moment.

"He's mine," Parker said, grinning.

Alex brought a hand to her chest and gasped. "Spencer?"

"Yep. The two stragglers behind him are my sister and her new boyfriend."

"Wow." Alex eyed the small boy, his eyes bright as he swung his arms in the air. “He is so adorable.”

Spencer stopped in front of them, breathing hard, with something in his hand. “Is this the lady, Daddy?”

Parker bent at the waist. “Yep. This is the pretty lady who saved me.”

Alex still had a hand on her chest, but she was certain not a soul on earth could wipe the smile from her face. “Hello, Spencer. I am so happy to meet you.” She extended her hand after a few seconds, not sure what protocol was for a boy his age. But Spencer latched on and gave her hand a firm shake, then offered her what was in his other closed hand, dangling it at arm’s length.

“What’s this?” She opened her

palm, still smiling, as she glanced at Parker, then back at Spencer.

He dropped a shell into her hand. “It’s for you.”

“Thank you very much.” She examined the small conch shell. “It’s lovely.”

Spencer’s twinkling blue eyes, the same color as his father’s, met Alex’s. He blinked a few times as a questioning expression filled his sweet face.

“Are you having Christmas by the sea?”

Warmth filled Alex’s soul. She hadn’t heard anyone ever use that phrase, besides her father. “Yes, I guess you could say I am.”

Spencer scratched his nose as he found his father’s gaze. “Maybe we can have Christmas by the sea with Alex sometime."

Parker and Alex exchanged glances, both smiling. Parker said, "I think I'd like that Spencer."

Alex nodded, and Spencer skipped away toward Parker's sister and boyfriend. Parker put his arm around Alex and pulled her close, both of them looking out across the ocean, soaking in the majestic feel of the sea.

And somehow, without a doubt, Alex knew that there would be many more Christmases by the sea. With Parker. And Spencer.

■ ■ ■ ■

An Amish Christmas Gift

■ ■ ■ ■

To Diana and Terry

GLOSSARY

ach: oh
daed: dad
danki: thank you
Englisch: those who are not Amish; the English language
Gott: God
gut: good
haus: house
kaffi: coffee
kinner: children
lieb: love
maed: girl
mamm: mom

mei: my
mudder: mother
nee: no
Ordnung: written and unwritten rules in an Amish district
rumschpringe: running around time for teenagers, beginning at 16 years old
Ya: yes

Chapter 1

Hannah King wished she could skip Christmas this year even though she'd always treasured the holiday and everything it represented. She forced herself to wrap gifts while her children spent time at their aunt and uncle's house on this crisp December morning. The aroma of freshly baked bread hung in the air, orange embers crackled as they shimmied up the fireplace, and she'd organized the children's presents from where she sat on her living room floor — just like she'd done every year. She was surrounded by various rolls of wrapping paper, colorful bows she'd made from ribbon purchased at the market, and an assortment of boxes.

As was tradition, they wouldn't have a Christmas tree, but Hannah would place the wrapped gifts around the living room to create a festive atmosphere. She'd already laid out garland atop the fireplace mantel and placed poinsettias on either side of the stone structure while her two daughters helped decorate other areas. Lillian, who had just turned seven, had attached red bows on the porch columns outside and created a lovely centerpiece for the dining room table using pinecones, red and green ribbons, and holly. Eighteen-year-old Mae had unpacked other decorations they kept stored in the basement and placed them around the house. Hannah hoped that being with her sister's family for the day might infuse some holiday joy into her daughters' lives.

Ruth and Henry didn't have children of their own yet, and they doted on Hannah's girls. Spoiled them was more like it. And that was okay with Hannah. It was their first Christmas without Paul, her beloved husband and father of the two beautiful girls. A life taken much too early.

Hannah slipped the pink sweater

she'd knitted for Lillian into a box. Her youngest daughter could still get away with wearing pastel colors at her age, and pink was Lillian's favorite color. She chose red and white striped wrapping paper, but she hadn't even closed the box when she covered her face with both hands and cried, the type of sobbing that people do only when they are alone. Her grief shook her to the core and often came on unexpectedly. Hannah did her best to stay strong for Lillian and Mae and never showed her emotions around them. She hadn't cried in front of anyone since the funeral, not even her sister, to whom she'd always been close. It was her job, as a mother, to be strong for her girls, and feigning strength around everyone else was good practice, albeit difficult.

Today, she needed the release, and shipping the girls to Ruth and Henry was about more than just needing privacy to wrap presents. She needed the solitude to let go of some of the grief that had such a firm hold on her, a type of suffocation that left her feeling as though she couldn't breathe sometimes. Hopefully, she could get it out of her system before the girls returned. It had been six months since the accident that took her husband's life at only forty-one years old. She couldn't help but wonder if she would always feel the stabbing pain in her chest that represented the void in her life.

Mae enjoyed being with her Aunt Ruth and Uncle Henry. Even though they had loved her father, she supposed it was easier for them to get on with life than it was for Mae, her sister, and her mother. There was a giant hole in their hearts, and even with all the Christmas decorations at home, the absence of their father, the void, the changes, the sadness . . . it hovered in the air like a dark cloud that would never produce rain or go away. The worst part was hearing her mother crying herself to sleep every night, only to pretend everything was okay when she was around Mae and her sister. Lillian was only seven and didn't have as many memories to hold onto as Mae. But after twenty years of marriage, it was her mother who seemed to be suffering the most, and it scared Mae.

Amish funerals were a sober affair but showing grief in public was discouraged. As was tradition, Mae's father had been buried three days after his death. Preceding the burial, a viewing was held at their home, followed by a church service, and then her father was laid to rest in the Amish cemetery, his headstone identical to all the others. Mae's mother had remained stoic and hadn't cried throughout any of the services even though Lillian and Mae shed tears, along with several others. Maybe her mother should have let go of some of her emotions. Was all that grief bottled up inside and spilling out privately at night? How long would her mother suffer? *Forever?*

Mae stood at the window and watched her uncle push Lillian on the swing when her aunt came up beside her.

"How's your *mamm*?" Aunt Ruth was three years younger than her mother, a beautiful woman with auburn hair and green eyes. She told everyone she must be adopted because there wasn't a redhead anywhere in the family tree. Mae's grandparents laughed at the notion and assured everyone Ruth wasn't adopted.

"She's okay." Mae hadn't told anyone that she often heard her mother softly crying late at night. With each new day, she prayed that her mom wouldn't suffer so much. Even though she fought hard to hide it, Mae could see the sadness in her mother's eyes, her daily interactions, and especially during worship service. Maybe the Spirit moved her. Perhaps she begged God to bring back her husband and Lillian and Mae's father.

Her Aunt Ruth put a hand on her back, rubbing gently. "I know it doesn't feel like it right now, but time will ease the pain, and eventually you will all be happy again." She paused, sighing. "Your *daed* was a *gut* man."

Mae's bottom lip trembled. She wasn't as good as her mother when it came to hiding her emotions.

"Look at those two." Aunt Ruth lowered her arm from Mae's back and pointed out the window. "He's going to make a wonderful *daed* someday."

Coming here was an escape from the sadness at her house, and her aunt must have sensed that Mae didn't want to talk about the loss they'd suffered.

Her aunt and uncle had been trying to have a baby for over ten years. There was no medical reason they shouldn't be able to, according to the doctor. Mae had heard about fertility drugs and in vitro fertilization, but most of their people — her aunt and uncle included — believed conception was in God's hands. "And you'll be a wonderful *mudder,*" Mae said as she turned to her and smiled.

"We will see." Aunt Ruth spoke with an air of hope marred by a dose of doubt as she grabbed Mae's hand and led her toward the kitchen. "Since we have some time to ourselves, I want to hear about this new boyfriend you have. I mean, I've known the Byler's for years, but it seems like Johnny turned into a man overnight." She pulled out a kitchen chair and motioned for Mae to sit. "I'll pour us some *kaffi,* and I made banana bread this morning."

"He goes by John now, not

Johnny." Mae reached for a slice of warm bread after her aunt set two plates and a platter on the table, then she returned with two cups of coffee.

"Your *mamm* said you two are spending a lot of time together." She smiled. "Do you think *John* is the one?"

Mae had gone out with two other boys after she'd turned sixteen and her parents allowed her to date. Each relationship had only lasted a few months and never progressed past a kiss on the cheek. John was different, and deep inside, Mae knew he was the one for her. She'd known him all her life, but his family lived outside of Montgomery. The town in southern Indiana was small, but John, his parents, and siblings were still part of the same district as Mae and her family. But due to the distance between their homes, she hadn't really gotten to know him until he began working at the lumberyard near her house. They had been seeing each other for three months, ever since she'd gone to the lumberyard to pick up supplies for small repairs needed on their house. She and John had slipped into an easy conversation, and before she left, he had asked her out for supper.

"I don't know if he is the one." Mae swallowed hard. She disliked lying to anyone, especially someone she loved as much as Aunt Ruth. But telling her aunt the truth would cause more heartache for everyone. Mae had already let things get out of hand with John. "We haven't been seeing each other all that long."

Her aunt got a faraway look in her eyes, then smiled as she refocused on Mae. "I knew I *liebed* Henry and that he was the one for me by our third date."

Mae longed to tell her aunt that she'd fallen for John right away, too, but she only forced a smile. "I guess we will see how it goes."

Her aunt took a bite of bread, then dabbed her mouth with her napkin. "When do you see him again?"

"Tonight. He's coming over." Mae's heart fluttered at the

thought. Her mother would put Lillian to bed early, then disappear into her bedroom so Mae and John could sit on the couch in the living room and have some time alone. She appreciated her mother's efforts.

"It's supposed to snow." Aunt Ruth lifted her shoulders, grinning, as she clutched her coffee cup between her hands. "So romantic. A warm fire, maybe some hot cider, and your *mamm* will have the house decorated for Christmas. It sounds wonderful."

Mae envisioned the evening, and it would be exactly as her aunt described. She hoped she wouldn't hear her mother crying in her bedroom. She prayed that thoughts of her father wouldn't overtake her emotions and cloud the evening. Grief had stages. She'd read a book about it that Aunt Ruth had given her. Mae knew time would heal her, but she wasn't sure that was the case for her mother, who seemed stuck in a bad place, unable to get past the intense pain, evidenced by her unwillingness to even mention Mae's father and crying herself to sleep almost every night. She did her best to put on a good act during daylight hours by attempting to be cheerful, and Mae was pretty sure her younger sister bought into it, but Mae didn't. For a while, she had thought her mother was getting better. Or her mother had just been better at hiding her emotions during those interludes. Perhaps the holidays had caused her grief to resurface even more.

She forced the thoughts away and cleared her throat. “John is a wonderful man,” she finally said in response to her aunt’s comments. But she would lose him to another woman eventually because Mae had no plans to marry John Byler.

Chapter 2

John cranked up the battery-operated heater in his buggy, pulled his black coat snug around him before he took hold of the reins and backed up, anxious to arrive at Mae's house. She'd have a warm fire going, coffee or hot cider ready, and she'd already told him they had been decorating for Christmas. He wouldn't care if they met in a rundown barn in the woods if he was near her. Being in her arms was all the warmth he needed. But the ambiance she'd described would be the perfect setting for tonight since John had a special surprise for Mae.

Snow swirled in powdery circles like magic fairy dust leading him to his future wife. It was much too soon to propose, but he knew beyond a shadow of a doubt that Mae was the woman he wanted to marry then raise a family. Six children. Three boys and three girls. He smiled to himself as he pictured Mae and their children seated around a big table in the house John would build for them. He'd already purchased a two-acre tract for when the time came to build a home. He'd been saving his money since he'd started working at sixteen, for only two years, but it had been enough to put a down payment on the property.

He spent the rest of his journey daydreaming about the life he and Mae would have. Hopefully, next fall, after the harvest, they would get married.

Everything was blanketed in white by the time he arrived at Mae's house almost forty-five minutes later. He was used to the long buggy ride to work daily. It would have been easier to go straight from work to Mae's house, but he had chores to do at home before he could visit her in the evenings, which made for a lot of traveling. But he'd travel however far he had to so that he could spend time with her.

After he pulled on his black knit cap, he stepped out of the buggy and unhitched his horse, then led the stallion to the lean-to nearby. Mae had already put out fresh oats and water for the animal.

Dodging the snowfall put a spring in John's step as he jogged toward the house with his chin tucked and gloved hands cupped above his eyebrows. His breath clouded in front of him, but it was impossible not to notice the evening light reflecting off the flakes that created a vibrant landscape.

He was stepping out of his boots on the covered front porch when Mae opened the door, smiling.

John was sure his future bride

grew more beautiful with each passing day. Her light brown hair was tucked beneath her prayer covering. She'd told him it had grown past her waist, although he wouldn't see the long tresses until they were married. Maybe before, if they went swimming over the summer, or if she allowed him to see her hair down. Some Amish women, his mother being one of them, didn't reveal their hair until marriage. Others were more liberal about the tradition. John wasn't sure what Mae's feelings were on the subject.

"Hurry and get out of your coat. You must be freezing." She bounced up on her toes as she hugged herself to stay warm from the cold air he was letting in.

He slid out of his coat and shook it before draping it over his arm, then popped off his hat and gloves, shaking off as much snow as he could before crossing the threshold to hang the items on the rack inside.

Mae closed the door behind him, then gave him a quick hug. He glanced around the living room filled with holiday decorations as the smell of cinnamon filled his nostrils. They made their way to the fireplace, where he warmed his hands, anxious to cup her cheeks and gaze into her brown eyes before kissing her the way he had been for the past two months. Their first month together had consisted of hugs and kisses on the cheek, but things had evolved into more than a close friendship. They had shared their first passionate kiss behind the barn after worship service at the Lantz's house. He had longed to be in her arms from that moment on. She stayed in his heart and on his mind even when he wasn't with her.

He was glad to be alone with Mae. Lillian was most likely already in bed. But Hannah, Mae's mother, could be nearby. She mostly stayed to herself in her bedroom when John visited, but he wasn't going to kiss Mae until he knew for sure.

"*Mamm* is already in her bedroom," Mae said as she grinned. "She said to tell you hello."

John rubbed his hands together to make sure they were warm enough, then wasted no more time before he cupped Mae's cheeks, his eyes fixed on hers. Could she read his expression? Did she know how much he loved her? They hadn't said the words, but he could feel the intensity of her emotions when he covered her mouth with his in a kiss that always left him weak in the knees.

Tonight was the night . . . that John would tell Mae that he was in love with her.

Mae was lost in the euphoria of John's tender embrace, the way he held her face in his strong hands, and the exploratory way that he kissed her repeatedly. The crackling of the fire fueled the warmth in her heart, and she wished she could live in this moment forever.

Because it couldn't last.

She loved him so much it hurt sometimes, and when she wasn't with him, she longed to see him. It was a cross between agony and euphoria. She was pretty sure he felt the same way but admitting it to each other would change things. It would feel like a commitment. Maybe they were already emotionally committed but saying it aloud would solidify a future that Mae could only dream about.

She eased out of his arms, kissed him tenderly on the cheek, then nodded to the coffee table. "I've got hot cider and cinnamon rolls."

"Those look delicious. And the decorations are beautiful too."

"*Danki.* Now let's get some food in you."

On the nights he visited her, he confessed to missing supper with his family, saying he was anxious to get on the road to see her. Most of the Amish families Mae knew, hers included, ate their evening meal at five o'clock. She'd repeatedly asked him to come for supper and that they could eat later those nights. He insisted it would be too late for all of them to eat since he had to work until five. After traveling home and handling his chores, he didn't arrive at her house until almost seven, sometimes later. Mae had offered to heat up leftovers for him, also, but he said he just wanted to focus his attention solely on her. She always made sure to have plenty of snacks though.

After they were settled on the couch, he took a big bite of cinnamon roll. "These are the best I've ever had," he said after he'd swallowed.

Mae chuckled. "You say that about everything me or *Mamm* make for you to eat." She imagined all the meals they could share together if they were to get married and have a family, something she used to think she wanted.

When he rubbed his stomach and smiled, an indication he was full after eating four large cinnamon rolls, Mae picked up their plates. Sometimes, she had finger sandwiches or snacks, but John had a fondness for anything freshly baked and didn't mind having it for supper. It was a long ride for him to visit her, and she appreciated the fact he had repeatedly told her that he didn't mind making the journey. She at least wanted to make sure he left with a full tummy . . . even if it was cinnamon rolls or a finger food.

Her relationship with John had begun as a distraction for Mae. Not that she wasn't wildly attracted to him, but she'd feared the grief over losing her father would leave her never feeling happy again. No one could fill the void of losing her dad, but John provided her with an escape. She had never meant to fall in love with him.

She held her breath as the clock in the kitchen ticked, trying to hear if her mother was crying in the bedroom, but she probably wouldn't hear her from the kitchen. As badly as Mae felt, the loss of her father seemed to have paralyzed her mother emotionally, even though she tried not to show it in front of her daughters. In some ways, there was just a shell of her mother left, a woman who went through the life she was expected to live, but like a robot who didn't express emotion. It wasn't that Hannah King wasn't a good mother to her children, but she was absent. Gone. Like Mae and Lillian's father but in a different way.

She refocused on John when she rounded the corner and came back to the living room. Could he be any more handsome? His dark hair was cut in the traditional style. She'd heard the English call it a bowl cut but John's bangs were long and pushed to the side, and he had what the Amish called 'hat hair' from where his hat had been on his head all day. But it was his dark eyes that Mae could get lost in, and with only the light from the lantern and the glow of the fire, gold flecks twinkled in his brown eyes and grew brighter as he grew closer.

John Byler wasn't just handsome. He truly cared about people, and it showed in his everyday actions. Since Mae had been around him, she'd seen him carry an elderly English woman's bags to her car when she struggled with the weight of her purchases at the lumberyard. He'd given a homeless man twenty dollars after his friend advised him against it, saying the man might just use it to buy alcohol or drugs. John's response was, "Or food." Then he just smiled.

His tenderness extended much further than strangers and was apparent the most when he was around his loved ones. John had a large family, and Mae knew all of them since they attended the same worship services. She liked to think her people were good in nature overall, but John seemed to take his goodness to another level, and she loved that about him.

As he put an arm around her, snuggling closer, Mae wondered if her father would have approved of them being alone together in the living room. *Probably not.* But Mae suspected her mother would have convinced him that Mae was responsible and that John could be trusted.

Mae missed her mother.

In between snacking on cinnamon rolls and sipping cider, they chatted about their day. John had spent the afternoon doing inventory at the lumberyard, and Mae told him about her visit with her aunt and uncle. Then John became unusually quiet, wringing his hands together.

Slowly he turned to her, tucked a strand of loose hair behind her ear, nuzzled her neck, then gently brushed his lips against hers before they locked eyes.

"I have something to tell you, Mae King." He kissed the tip of her nose, and Mae stopped breathing. If it was what she thought it would be, then their time together would be coming to an end soon. "I can't hold it in any longer," he said in a whisper, the fire continuing to crackle, the clock ticking louder in Mae's mind.

Please don't. He would expect her to say it back, and she couldn't.

He gently took her cheeks into his

hands and gazed into her eyes. "Mae, I —"

She crushed her lips to his, causing their foreheads to knock together. Any discomfort from their heads bumping was quickly dissipating as Mae kissed him with all the passion she felt. Because she knew it would be the last time.

He eased her away and captured her eyes again as he tenderly clutched her shoulders. "Mae, I *lieb* you. I know we're young, and I know we've only been seeing each other for three months, but I am sure I am in *lieb* with you."

Mae chewed on her bottom lip as she avoided his eyes, casting them down as she reached up and twirled the string of her prayer covering.

She couldn't ignore him, and when she finally looked into his eyes, she saw his fear . . . fear that she didn't feel the same way.

"Danki," she finally said barely above a whisper. "That's nice of you to say," she added when his jaw dropped slightly, his eyes searching hers.

She stood abruptly. "Uh, I think I hear Lillian awake in her room. I should probably go check on her." It was a lie she would ask God to forgive later.

John slowly lifted himself from the couch and looped his thumbs beneath his suspenders. "*Ya,* I should probably go. It's getting late."

It wasn't late, and he didn't look at her as he moved toward the door and quickly dressed in his coat, hat, and gloves.

Mae could feel her heart cracking. But this was the kindest thing to do for John, to let him move on and fall in love with someone who wanted to have a life with him. He was right . . . they were young. They would both get over this even though the pain in Mae's chest felt unbearable, and she hoped she could hold off her tears until he was gone.

At the door, he kissed her on the cheek. "Bye, Mae."

"Bye," she mouthed, aware that no sound came out.

After the door between them closed, she pressed her head to the wood and laid her hands flat against the surface on either side of her head. She didn't want to cry, but tears spilled down her cheeks just the same.

Then she heard a familiar sound coming from her mother's bedroom. Quiet whimpering.

Mae wanted to burst through her mother's bedroom door, climb into bed with her, and hold her tightly, to comfort her. Maybe it should be the other way around, but as badly as Mae was hurting, it was worse for her mother. Mae was never going to allow herself to love the way her mother had loved her father. She'd never survive the pain if she lost a husband, and she'd end up in constant agony like her mother.

She padded up the stairs, stopping to check on Lillian who was sound asleep, then she ran to her room and waited until she was behind her bedroom door before she pressed her face into her pillow and sobbed.

Chapter 3

John felt like he'd been punched in the gut the entire way home, his stomach twisting and churning with humiliation. How could he have misread Mae's feelings for him and embarrassed himself the way he did? He would have never told her he loved her if he hadn't been sure of her feelings. But he'd been wrong, and the awkwardness of the exchange made him not want to face her ever again, which would be impossible. He would see her at least twice a month at worship service. He doubted she would visit him at the lumberyard anymore or invite him to her house. Her flushed face and the way she'd avoided his eyes expressed how uncomfortable his admission had been for her.

By the time he got home, he had a knot in his throat the size of a walnut. He couldn't remember the last time he'd cried, but his eyes were moist as he made his way up the porch steps, praying his parents and three sisters were asleep. If anyone spoke to him right now, he feared he couldn't mask his emotions, and that would top off his already humiliating night in the worst way.

He clicked on the flashlight in his pocket and shined it at his feet as he tiptoed up the stairs. Luckily, he made it to his bedroom without any confrontations, and after quietly closing the door behind him, he shuffled to his bed, clicked off the flashlight, and sat in the dark, feeling defeated. How could he have miscalculated Mae's feelings for him so badly, he wondered again?

Eventually, he lit the oil lantern on his nightstand and lay atop his bed, thinking about the past few months with Mae. Their relationship had grown so naturally, even though there wasn't anything seemingly natural about what happened tonight.

She led me on. The more he

thought about it, his heartbreak began turning to anger. Maybe he was just filling a void in her life, helping her get through this first year without her father. He would have been happy to do that, but every mutual indication had led to a romantic relationship. It seems she wouldn't have let it get to that point if she didn't care about him. Maybe she did care for him, maybe even a lot . . . but she didn't love him, or she would have said so.

His ponderings continued as he bathed in the upstairs bathroom he shared with his siblings, then dressed for bed. He tiptoed barefoot to his bedroom, hoping not to wake up anyone since he was bathing later than normal. He scrambled to the propane heater and turned it up before he snuggled beneath the covers. Despite his continuous yawns, he couldn't turn off his mind, and every time he pictured Mae's face when he'd told her he loved her, he wanted to cry, then the bitterness returned.

It was around midnight when Mae woke up suddenly. There was a crash downstairs, and as she fumbled for the flashlight on her nightstand, she slipped into her robe, then scurried down the steps toward movement she heard in the kitchen.

Mae rushed to where her mother stood trembling but stopped abruptly when she saw broken glass surrounding her mother's bare feet.

"Mamm?" She shined the light at her own feet. She hadn't taken the time to put on socks or slippers. She was inches away from the broken glass pitcher her mother kept by her bed, made obvious by the large, cracked handle among the tinier shards. "Are you hurt?"

"*Nee,* I'm so sorry I woke you." Her mother's eyes were glazed, her face cast in a dull pallor as her bottom lip trembled. "I came to get more water, and I dropped the pitcher."

At that moment, her mother looked and spoke like a child who was frightened and in trouble.

"Don't move." Mae pushed her palm toward her mother to drive the point home. She edged her way to the kitchen door that led outside and slipped into her mother's rubber boots before grabbing the broom and dustpan.

"Glass crunched beneath the rubber soles as she grew closer to where her mother was standing. "Here." She handed her mother the flashlight and wondered why her mother hadn't used a flashlight to get to the kitchen. Maybe because it was a straight shot from her downstairs bedroom, through the den, and into the kitchen.

As her mother stood shaking, Mae swept the glass into the dustpan and dumped it in the trashcan. "Don't move," she said again, and her mother groggily nodded.

Mae went into the den and retrieved another pair of her mother's shoes. "Slip into these." She laid the shoes on the wooden floor in front of her mother. "It's too dark to see if I got all the glass. I'll try to be up before Lillian to double-check in the morning."

"I-I don't know what happened." Her mom shrugged, her lip still trembling. "It just slipped out of *mei* hand." She rubbed Mae's shoulders. "*Danki* for tending to the mess. I'm so sorry I woke you up," she said again as a touch of color returned to her face.

"It's okay. Since we're up, do you want me to make us some hot cocoa or — ?"

"*Nee.* I should get back to bed.

The sun will be up early, and I have much to do tomorrow." Her mother seemed to force a smile before she kissed Mae on the cheek.

Mae watched her as she shuffled back to her bedroom with Mae's flashlight shining at her feet. The mother she used to have would have noticed Mae's eyes were swollen and insisted they chat about what was ailing her.

As her mother's bedroom door clicked shut, Mae stood in the darkness since her mother had left with her flashlight. She finally slipped out of the heavy rubber boots, returning them to the designated area right outside the door, then she started back to the stairs, hoping she wouldn't step on a sliver of glass she might have missed.

Moonlight mixed with the glowing cinders from the fire and filled the living room with shadowy images. Mae pictured her father sitting in his favorite recliner to her left, his glasses low on his nose as he read the latest edition of *The Budget* newspaper. Then her eyes drifted to her mother's knitting basket next to the rocking chair in the corner, and she envisioned her mother quietly humming as she worked on her latest project. Her mother still knitted, but she hadn't heard the comfort of her sweet, wordless tunes since her father died.

In the still of the night, the clock

on the mantel ticked, an owl hooted outside, and when she shifted her gaze to the window, moon rays reflected off the lightly falling snow. Despite the festive decorations and wrapped gifts, a tear rolled down her cheek as she looked at the couch. The look on John's face when she hadn't told him she loved him might haunt her forever. She recalled her aunt telling her that time would heal the grief about her father. Would time also heal a broken heart?

She heard her mother's quiet whimpers and doubted her aunt's words. Mae was filled with grief about her father, but her mother's heart was broken in a different way, and now Mae's was too.

Night after night, Mae heard her mother's soft cries, and she respected her privacy. But tonight, she padded her way to the downstairs bedroom and knocked. *"Mamm?"*

Silence.

"*Mamm,* are you awake?" Mae put her ear against the door but heard no reply. She turned to walk away, her heart sinking even more, then the door opened.

"I'm sorry. I took off with this." Her mother handed her the flashlight that she had pointed to the floor, lighting up Mae's toes. "You didn't step on any glass, did you?" her mom asked from where she stood in her bedroom, the door partially opened and clearly not an invitation to come inside.

Mae took the flashlight and shook her head. "*Nee,* I didn't step on glass. I-I just . . ." She shrugged. "I just wanted to see if you were okay." Did her mother hear the tremble in her voice? Would she wrap her arms around her to comfort her? Did she recognize the emotions of others the way she used to, always attuned to her loved ones' needs?

"*Ya, ya.* I'm fine." Her mother smiled, but Mae could tell it was forced. And as much as she hated to hear her mother crying night after night, she wished she would share her emotions with Mae, so that in turn, Mae could share hers. Maybe together they could lift some of each other's burdens. "Go back to bed, Mae. Morning will be here soon enough."

Mae didn't move as the door closed. Maybe her mother didn't see her trembling lip, her need to have a mom again, even at her age. Or maybe she just didn't care anymore.

Hannah leaned her head against the door until she heard her oldest daughter walk away. Mae was hurting, and Hannah had seen her daughter's bottom lip trembling as she blinked back tears. She had wanted nothing more than to embrace her, to tell her that their grief would get better with time. At least, that's the adage she'd heard so many times, but she wasn't strong enough for that. It took all her effort to contain her emotions in front of the girls. If she'd let Mae into her bedroom, cuddled her like she did when she was a child, kissed her on the cheek . . . Hannah would have fallen apart. That was not something an eighteen-year-old should have to witness.

She crawled back under her sheets, then snuggled into the Amish wedding quilt that had been a gift from her sister and several others in their quilting group. As she gingerly ran her hand across the intricate details, rings with all her favorite pastel colors, she closed her eyes and pictured Paul lying next to her. But when she reached over to his side of the bed, of course, he wasn't there. The bed felt huge, like the hole in her heart. Even in her grief, she needed to make a mental note to do a better job of stifling her late-night sobs. Mae might have heard her crying and triggered her daughter's emotions. In Hannan's mind, she had to believe they would all recover from the loss of their husband and father.

But when?

How long will it take?

She prayed constantly for the healing powers only God could provide. Through her relationship with Jesus, she had begged for comfort for all of them. Tonight, she said extra healing prayers for

Mae and Lillian as they faced their first Christmas without their father. And she asked God to give her the strength to maintain a sense of normalcy when she was around her girls. It was exhausting to hold in her emotions until she was alone at night, but if she showed strength and resolve to get through this first holiday season as a widow, then it would hopefully carry over to her daughters, especially Mae. *Widow.* The word still sounded strange in her mind, and she wasn't sure she'd ever spoken it aloud.

Hannah drifted off the same way she did every night, with tears in her eyes and clutching Paul's pillow, aware of the emptiness in the bed . . . and in her heart.

Chapter 4

The weeks of December marched on for John, and he was glad he had work to keep his mind occupied most of the time. The Advent season should have been festive, but when thoughts of Mae pushed to the forefront of his mind, he had a hard time getting into the spirit of the season.

He took note of the red ribbons tied to evergreen trees here and there on the way to the Schrock's home and the way the snow blanketed everything around them, glistening in the early morning light. One of his sisters had attached a bell on the back of the buggy, and it jingled in rhythm with the horse's hooves. His heart was too heavy to embrace the anticipation such images and sounds should have brought on.

John guided the covered buggy to worship service with the eldest of his sisters, Sarah, who was a year younger than John. She'd insisted on riding with him alone, meaning she had something on her mind. His younger sisters, Rebecca and Anna — eight and twelve — traveled with their parents in a separate buggy.

Sarah cleared her throat. *Here*

it comes.

"There's a rumor going around that you and Mae aren't seeing each other anymore," Sarah said before they were even on the main road that led to the Schrock's home where the service would be held today. "And I've noticed that you haven't been to her *haus* in almost two weeks."

John briefly glared at his sister. He would have to face Mae today, and he hadn't seen her since his last trip to her house. She also hadn't visited the lumberyard since then. "It didn't work out."

Sarah was the romantic in the family, always with her head in a book about couples in love, and she had a huge crush on one of the guys who worked at the lumberyard. John assumed it was mutual based on Aaron's interactions with his sister. But John had assumed a lot lately, specifically that Mae loved him. He hoped neither Sarah nor Aaron stomped on each other's heart the way Mae had his.

Distance from her had only fueled his confusion. At the least, she owed him an explanation. Every time he pondered the situation, he was sure that she had acted equally as in love with him as he was with her. *Acted.* That's what she'd done.

"Why didn't it work out?" Sarah bounced in her seat when John flicked the reins, sped up, and hit a pothole in the road.

"She just wasn't the right woman

for me." The truth was, Mae was the perfect woman for him. He was apparently the wrong guy for her though. John and Sarah mostly got along, but he wasn't going to share his humiliation with her.

"Hmm . . . I thought for sure that you would end up marrying her." She shrugged. "I don't know her all that well, but I like her. We've attended several quilting parties hosted by mutual friends, and of course, I see her every two weeks at worship." She tapped a finger to her chin. "So . . . who broke up with who?"

John worried that his love for Mae would bubble to the surface, and the only way to contain his emotions was to allow indifference to take over. "It's none of your business. Can you just let it go?" His voice was harsher than he'd intended.

Sarah scowled. "You don't have to be so mean about it."

John sighed, knowing his words were misdirected. "I'm sorry, Sarah. I just don't want to talk about it."

Sarah turned to face him with an eyebrow raised. "*Ach,* I see. She broke up with you."

John resisted the urge to speak to her unkindly by taking a deep breath. "No one really broke up with anyone. It just . . ." He searched for a truthful explanation. ". . . fizzled out, I guess." *And left a giant hole in my heart.*

Sarah was quiet. "I'm sorry," she said barely above a whisper.

John swallowed back a lump in his throat, and they were quiet the rest of the ride.

Mae had the reins as she and her mother, and Lillian traveled to worship service. She was nervous to see John after cutting off things between them so abruptly.

Her mother adjusted the battery-operated heater on the dashboard of the buggy. "I noticed John hasn't come to the *haus,*" she said, as if reading Mae's mind. Long buggy rides had always prompted her mother to be more talkative than in their day-to-day interactions around the house, although today,

Mae wished that wasn't the case. "And, to *mei* knowledge, you haven't visited him at the lumberyard. Did something happen between the two of you?"

Mae knew her mother would eventually ask why John wasn't courting her anymore. And apparently, she couldn't read minds after all, or she'd know why. "He just wasn't the right person for me." She held her breath. They might not be able to read minds, but parents could usually spot a lie.

Her mother peered at her as her eyebrows narrowed. "I'm surprised to hear that. I thought you might be in *lieb* with him."

If Mae let this conversation go on much longer, she'd be a blubbering mess by the time they arrived at worship service. She shrugged. *"Nee."*

"Hmm . . ." her mother responded as she refocused on the road in front of them.

Mae's stomach churned with nervous anxiety about seeing John. She prayed her mother would drop the subject.

Lillian sneezed from where she was seated in the backseat. "Tissue! I need a tissue, please."

Their mother began rummaging through her purse until she found a travel pack of Kleenex, quickly handing it over her shoulder to Lillian. After blowing her nose, Lillian said she was cold. The battery-operated heater was on as high as it would go, and they all had heavy blankets wrapped around them. Mae was warm in the covered buggy.

Her mother twisted around and put a hand to Lillian's head. "I think you might have a little fever."

"Then let's skip church." Lillian slapped her hands to her knees. "I'm sick."

Mae felt an adrenaline rush of hope surge through her, followed by a wave of guilt. She usually enjoyed the service, but today, she'd be relieved to miss it. Lillian whined every other Sunday about going to church, but at seven years old, three hours was a long time to sit still.

"Let's just see how you do. If you

start feeling bad, we can leave early." Her mother handed Mae's younger sister the travel pack of Kleenex. "Keep these in the pocket of your apron in case you need one."

Lillian did as she was told, and Mae's body tensed when the Schrock's house came into view. It was a smaller crowd than usual, but sometimes the older folks couldn't get out in the weather when it was this cold and snowing, as was the case with both sets of Mae's grandparents. Mae had hoped it would be a full house, easier to stay out of view and away from John.

After Mae tethered the horse to the fencepost, she scurried to catch up to her mother and Lillian, then rushed across the threshold as they began shedding their heavy coats, black bonnets, and snow boots. After Mae placed her boots atop the pile and found space on the long rack by the door for her coat and bonnet, she padded toward the kitchen in her socks, prepared to help with the meal that would be served after worship service. Her mother was by her side. Lillian ran off to find children her age. She didn't look sick to Mae, and Mae didn't want her sister to feel bad, but she didn't want to stay for the entire service, especially the meal when everyone would be wandering and socializing.

The kitchen was full of women shuffling around in their socks, but

Mae and her mother left the room when Nellie Schrock said they had everything under control.

Mae spotted John across the room talking with a woman about Mae's age — the beautiful and highly sought-after Bethany Troyer. Her stomach lurched as she stopped in her tracks and stared at them. Her mother kept going and fell into a conversation with Aunt Ruth. Mae remained frozen and unable to look away from John and Bethany, especially when Bethany laughed, put her hand on John's arm, and flashed her pearly white teeth at him. Bethany had huge green eyes and beautiful blonde hair that would often escape in ringlets from her prayer cap. Mae had always wondered why John had never courted Bethany the way everyone else in their district had done. No one had snagged her yet. Maybe she'd been waiting for John to pursue her.

As the knot in her throat grew larger, she blinked back tears. She couldn't have meant much to John if he'd already moved on to someone else. Her tears turned to anger almost right away when John whispered something in Bethany's ear before he touched her arm and walked away. Bethany smiled, then John looked right at Mae and locked eyes with her for a couple of seconds before walking in the opposite direction from where she was standing.

Jealousy was a sin, but it wrapped around Mae like a serpent, squeezing the life out of her as her stomach roiled and her heart burned with a betrayal she wasn't justified to have. Mae was the one who hadn't responded to John's admission that he loved her. She was the one who hadn't visited him at the lumberyard or invited him to her house. Their relationship's demise was her fault, and that's what she wanted.

Or so she thought.

Why was her heart putting up such a fight?

This wasn't the time or place to try to make sense of that battle. Instead, she needed to stay strong and make it through the service.

Resolving, then, to listen to her head and not her heart, she pursed her lips and gritted her teeth so hard she had to be careful not to crack a tooth.

It was easy for John to avoid Mae during the worship service since the men sat on one side facing the women in the Schrock's den with the bishop and elders in the middle of the room. He tried not to look at her, but occasionally he couldn't help himself and glanced at her. Not once did he catch her looking in his direction. But he had captured her glare when he'd talked to Bethany earlier. He had seen Mae enter the room, and John intentionally flirted with Bethany, even though he hadn't ever been interested in her. She was pretty, and lots of guys his age ogled her and tried to date her, but she wasn't John's type. Even though she was beautiful, she was too giggly, gossiped a lot, and only one woman held his heart.

John knew what Mae's anger looked like. He'd only seen it once while they were in town eating a burger. Mae had looked out the window by their booth just in time to see a man kick a stray dog. She jumped from her seat holding her plate before John could stop her. She scurried outside and yelled at the man, who only shrugged before he walked away, then Mae gave the starving animal the rest of her burger after removing the onions and ultimately found the dog a good home.

The only other time he'd seen her face turn that red and her eyes blaze with anger was before the service when he'd caught her looking at him flirting with Bethany. He should have felt good about it, that she was jealous. A part of him wanted to hurt her the way she'd hurt him. But he couldn't make another person love him. He reminded himself that she'd played the part well, though, and had led him on.

When the service was over, John realized he had spent most of his time analyzing what had happened between him and Mae, and he'd missed most of what the bishop talked about. He would need to ask forgiveness during devotions this evening, for allowing himself to be distracted. But even as the congregation stood and people began to mingle, John's eyes roamed the room in search of Mae.

Where is she?

Had she sprinted ahead of the other women to get to the kitchen and help prepare the meal?

It wasn't until after most of the women were in the kitchen that he saw her standing alone by herself near the hallway entrance. He waited to see if she was going down the hall to the bathroom, but she didn't move, and she had a hand across her stomach. When her lips began to tremble, John's heart pounded in his chest as he spontaneously moved toward her. He couldn't get to her fast enough. She might not love him, but even distance couldn't keep him from loving her. And something was wrong.

CHAPTER 5

Mae's feet were rooted to the floor even though she wanted to run away. She'd allowed her emotions to take over as if her feelings were a runaway train she couldn't control. No matter the circumstances and her fears about commitment, she'd had three hours to think about a life without John, barely hearing most of what the bishop said. It had been ample time for her moods to flip-flop between anger about Bethany . . . and regret.

She'd ultimately ended up feeling more regret than anger.

As John approached her, she held her breath. In the distance, she could see her mother watching her, with eyebrows drawn and eyes questioning.

"Are you okay?" John tilted his head slightly as his eyes reflected sincere concern.

"I-I . . ." Mae didn't think she could speak without crying. Standing in the middle of the room, she could feel more people looking at them amid the quiet chatter. A few folks had already moved out to the barn where heaters warmed the space they would soon use to share a meal. "Sorry." She lowered her head. It was all she could manage to say, and it was how she felt. Elaborating would only make things worse.

"Can we go somewhere and talk?" John gazed into her eyes the familiar way she'd only seen in her dreams lately, and she wanted nothing more than to throw her arms around him and tell him how much she loved him.

"I can't." She wanted to keep her head down, but she eventually raised her eyes to his. "I mean, I'm expected to help with the meal."

"Then can we talk after the meal?" John's eyes pleaded with her, and they couldn't go on like this forever. She would tell him that she cared about him very much, that she was sorry that she had let things go on for as long as she had, and apologize for leading him on.

"Okay." She wasn't sure she'd be able to eat anything, but it would give her time to organize her thoughts.

She slowly edged around him when her mother motioned for her to come her way. Lillian was at her side now.

"I'm sorry to do this because I saw you talking with John, but Lillian is for sure running a fever." Her mother was holding her little sister's hand. "I think we need to go. I'll find us something to eat at home."

"Mae-Mae, I don't feel *gut.*" Lillian tugged on Mae's dress with her free hand.

Saved. Mae hated that her sister was sick, but for today, she would be able to avoid a more detailed conversation with John.

"It's okay, Lillian. Really." She felt her sister's forehead. "*Ya,* she's pretty warm."

"I already told Nellie that we were going to sneak out. She gave me some children's Tylenol for Lillian, but she understood that I wanted to get her home and tucked into bed." She motioned for Mae to follow her toward the front door where they stopped and bundled up like everyone else was doing before heading to the barn. "I should have told your Aunt Ruth, but I couldn't find her or your uncle."

Mae untethered the horse, then got the heater going while her mother covered up Lillian with an extra blanket in the backseat.

She backed up the buggy and got on the road without looking toward the crowd in the barn, afraid she would see John through one of the two opened doors, which might cause her to cry. She wasn't doing that.

Mae's mother waited until Lillian had dozed off in the backseat before she said anything. "I saw you talking to John. Did that go well?"

Her mother was a professional at hiding her emotions. Mae would have to learn from her. Might as well practice now. She cleared her throat, blowing a breath of cold air in front of her. “We didn’t have time to say much. But it’s fine. It doesn’t matter.”

“Um . . .” Her mother snuggled into the blanket she had around her. “By the look on both of your faces, it appeared to matter.”

Mae fought the urge to lash out at her mother. Suddenly, she was present and available. Where had she been since their father died? *“Mamm . . .”* She took a deep breath, reminding herself of the endless nights her mother cried herself to sleep. Mae didn’t have the heart to add to her suffering. *“Mamm,”* she said in a gentler voice. “John told me he *liebed* me.”

For the first time since her father died, her mother smiled a real and genuine smile as she pressed her palms together and closed her eyes. "How wonderful." She opened her eyes and turned to Mae. "Falling in *lieb* is a wonderful thing."

Mae wanted to say — *Is it? Because it will destroy you if that person dies.* Instead, she said, "*Mamm,* I already told you that John is not the man for me. I don't *lieb* him." Saying the lie aloud caused her chest to tighten.

Her mother's expression fell. "Are you sure? Because all the time when he was at the *haus,* all your visits to —"

"*Ya,* I'm sure. I don't *lieb* him and dragging it out would have only made things worse." She hated lying to her mother, but even more so, she disliked robbing her mother of the real contentment she seemed to feel at the thought of Mae and John being in love. And she still hadn't explained anything to John. Deep down, she knew he deserved an explanation, but she was glad it wasn't happening today.

They were quiet the rest of the way home.

John couldn't believe Mae had left with her mother and sister before the meal. Had she purposefully avoided talking to him by convincing her family to leave early? Frustration roared in his hungry stomach, but his appetite had left him when he saw Mae pull away in the buggy.

He picked at his food out in the barn, but as soon as he was done, he made his way to the kitchen where he found Mae's aunt. "Ruth, can I talk to you for a minute?"

She wiped her hands on a kitchen towel, then followed John to the mud room. "Why did your sister leave with Mae and Lillian before the meal? Is everything okay?" He tried to keep the desperation he felt out of his question.

Ruth shrugged. "As far as I know, everything is all right." She scratched her cheek. "It's unlike them, though, to leave without saying anything, especially before they even ate. I'll call Hannah from *mei* cell phone when I get home. I forgot to bring it."

John had never wanted a cell phone more than he did right now. The bishop allowed cell phones for emergencies and business use. John's parents didn't approve of the devices, and said it was an abused privilege. Technically, John could have bucked up to his folks since he was in his *rumschpringe,* but while he was under their roof, he mostly respected their rules — at least the ones they felt strongly about such as the use of mobile phones.

"I'm sure everything is fine." Ruth tapped him on the arm before giving him an all-knowing half-smile. Surely, Mae's aunt was aware that he and Mae hadn't spent any time together recently. He wanted to broach the subject, but it felt awkward, and she was gone before he had the chance to come up with a question that didn't sound desperate.

Luckily Sarah was ready to go home shortly after the meal, and he was grateful that she didn't ask him any more questions about Mae. John's mind was already on overdrive. He supposed he could go to Mae's house to make sure everyone was all right, but she'd been so hesitant to even talk to him, that he was nervous to approach her again. He was just going to have to accept that it was over. It had been a wonderful three months, but if he ever fell in love again — which he doubted — he would proceed with a lot more caution.

Mae prepared chicken soup and turkey sandwiches while her mother tended to Lillian, whose fever still hadn't broken.

"She's tucked into bed," her mother said as she walked into the kitchen. "I'll take her some soup if she doesn't feel like coming downstairs soon."

"I hope she doesn't have the flu." Mae stirred the soup atop the stove. "Christmas is only a week away."

Her mother sat at the kitchen table. "I hope not too."

She looked over her shoulder just in time to see her mom yawning. "*Mamm,* why don't you go take a nap. I can check on Lillian and take her some soup."

"Nee." Her mother grinned, which was nice to see. "I'm hungry, and somehow your chicken soup is always better than mine, which is odd since I taught you to make it, and it's *mei* recipe."

That was twice that Mae had seen her mother smile today. Real smiles, not the kind she put on for show. Mae would have felt more hopeful about her mom's grief getting a little better if she didn't feel so miserable herself. She missed her father terribly, but whatever this heartbreak was that she was feeling for John was different. She couldn't control what happened to her father, but she could control her own love life. And under different circumstances, she'd be crying on her mother's shoulder. She would stay hopeful that her mother was slowly returning to her and Lillian, but she wasn't going to add her burdens to her mother's overwhelming grief.

"Here you go." She placed a bowl of soup in front of her mother, along with half of a turkey sandwich, prepared the way she liked with just turkey, mustard, and pickles. "And I'm sure the soup doesn't taste better than yours."

Her mother blew on a spoonful before tasting the soup. "*Ya,* it's better than mine. You're putting some secret ingredient in it." She pointed the spoon at her and giggled." It was like a beautiful melody, her laughter, and it soothed Mae's soul.

Something was changing. Mae wasn't sure why her mother's attitude had shifted, but it made the sting about John lessen, if only a little. She was careful not to think about him too much and would take that cue from her mother and wait until she was alone to let her emotions spill out. And she was sure she would tonight.

Chapter 6

For three nights in a row, Hannah heard Mae crying. Lillian had gotten over whatever bug had latched onto her, but Hannah had been checking on her nightly. Otherwise, she might not have known how upset her oldest daughter was. And she didn't know if it was grief about her father or about not seeing John, or a combination of it all. But Mae had always talked to her about things, and Hannah suspected that she hadn't been truthful about the end of her relationship with John.

Hannah had made it a point to be more cheerful during the day and to mute her own misery at night, sometimes successfully, and other times she still cried herself to sleep. But worrying about Mae took priority over her own grief right now.

Tonight, she knocked softly on Mae's door. "Mae, are you okay? Can I come in?"

She heard her daughter sniffle. "*Mamm,* I just want to be alone. Is that okay?"

Hannah's eyes filled with tears, but this time it was for her daughter, and not all she had lost. She opened her mouth to tell Mae that it wasn't okay and that she was coming in, but she reminded herself of all the times Mae had knocked on her door and asked if she was all right, asked if she could come in, and Hannah always said she wanted to be alone. For now, she would respect that. "Okay," she said softly. "But I'm here if you need me."

No answer.

Hannah hadn't been there as much as she could have been for her children. Their basic needs had been met, but she had emotionally checked out at certain times. Her girls deserved parental support now more than ever, especially with their first Christmas season minus Paul approaching, so she was going to work on being a better mother.

As she climbed back into bed, she reached her arm across the empty space where Paul used to sleep, but her grief over her husband wasn't shredding her insides as much as the thought of her daughter crying upstairs. Even though Hannah had been emotionally absent, it had seemed kinder than to cry in front of her children. Today, she had tried to be more emotionally attuned to her children, but still, her oldest daughter cried upstairs. She threw back the covers, sat up, and eased into her slippers, prepared to go upstairs and pull Mae into her arms. But, again, she thought of all the times Mae had tried to comfort her, and she had wanted to just be left alone. Sighing, she fluffed her pillows and laid down again. Tomorrow was Christmas Eve. She would try to be festive and make it a good day for Mae and Lillian.

Mae pulled her knees to her chest and snuggled into her down comforter as tears wet her pillow. It took everything she had not to run downstairs, crawl into bed with her mother, and let her mother stroke her hair the soothing way she did when Mae was a child. But Mae wasn't a child anymore. She was a grown woman . . . or maybe an almost-grown woman at eighteen.

As she faced her first Christmas without her father, she wondered what the next few days would be like. A normal Christmas Eve consisted of cooking all day long, her mother humming, Lillian shaking presents that were scattered throughout the house . . . and her father being particularly flirty with her mother. Her parents had always been affectionate, but something about Christmas seemed to bring out the best in all of them, and her father had been no exception.

Her parents loved each other deeply. Mae had always known that as far back as she could remember. If they quarreled — and Mae was sure they must have — it was never in front of her or Lillian. They had kissed a lot, and her mother would blush and playfully say, "Paul, not in front of the *kinner.*"

Mae longed for that kind of love with John, but it just wasn't worth taking a chance that something would happen to him. Memories of her father and Christmases past floated through her mind like a fog that might never lift, and within the denseness of her recollections, thoughts of John were lightning bolts within her storm of emotions. But she held her breath for a few seconds when she heard a noise in her sister's bedroom. It sounded like crying, and Mae moved quickly to get to her.

Mae didn't knock but flung open Lillian's door and within the shadows of darkness, she saw her sister sitting up in bed rubbing her eyes and choking back sobs.

She went to the bed, sat, and pulled Lillian into her arms. "Are you feeling sick?"

Her sister shook her head. *"Nee.* I miss *Daed."* Lillian cried harder.

Mae held her tighter. "I know you do, sweetheart." She stroked her sister's long brown hair, and again she recalled the way her mother used to do the same thing when Mae was hurting. Mae wondered how many times Lillian had cried herself to sleep. Mae had done so plenty of times since her father's death, but both she and Lillian functioned with a level of normality her mother didn't seem to have anymore . . . even though Mae had seen the rebirth of her mother a little today.

"Will you read me a story?" Lillian's voice cracked as she spoke, her tears spilling out against Mae's nightgown.

She eased her sister away, pushed loose strands of hair from her tiny face, then said, "*Nee,* I won't. But I have a better idea." She rummaged around on the nightstand until she found her sister's flashlight and clicked it on. She stood, lifted Lillian into her arms, gave her a tight squeeze, then set her down. Lillian wore thick socks to bed. Mae wished she'd taken the time to slide into her slippers as the cold floor sent a chill the length of her body. But she held Lillian's hand, and together they went downstairs, the smells of the season wafting up their nostrils as they neared the first floor. Cinnamon comingled with pine, and in the near darkness with only the flashlight on, Mae took in the colorful wrapped presents and decorations, and how it all represented the anticipatory feel of Christmases past.

Mae was almost dragging Lillian across the living room, then hesitated at her mother's bedroom door, listening . . . to her crying. But she didn't knock. She pushed the door open. *"Mamm."*

Her mother sprung to a sitting position, and Mae was able to make out her actions in the dark as she struggled to wipe away tears before she flipped on the flashlight she kept on her nightstand. She shined it right at Mae and Lillian, then gasped.

"*Mei maeds,* what's the matter? Why are you both crying?"

"We miss *Daed,*" Lillian said through her tears. She broke away from Mae and ran to her mother's open arms.

"I know you do, *mei* sweet girl." As her mother welcomed Lillian in her arms, gently rocking back and forth, stroking her hair, Mae stood in the doorway with tears rolling down her cheeks. She didn't need an invitation to join them, but she wanted one, and she didn't have to wait long. Her mother motioned for Mae to come in, and when she got into bed, her mother held them both, and together they all cried as if their father had died that very day, not six months ago. Their mother sobbed the hardest.

"I *lieb* you *maeds* so much," she said, her voice shaking with emotion. "I know you're hurting, but we will get through this first Christmas without your beloved *daed* as best we can."

"Together," Mae said softly as her mother stroked her hair in the same soul-soothing way she was doing with Lillian.

"*Ya,* together." Her mother pulled them both closer.

For the first time since the death of her husband, Mae and Lillian's mother wept openly, and showed true emotion, and even though sadness filled the room, there was also relief. Mae realized that now they could face Christmas together, not alone in solitude, faking emotions, and pretending everything was okay. As she embraced this new reality, a calmness began to settle over her, and she realized for the first time the true love of family that her father continued to gift them . . . even in his absence.

John was late for breakfast, which was a big no-no on Christmas Eve morning, and it would have been even worse if it had been Christmas Day. He would need to set the alarm on his battery-operated clock for tomorrow morning.

"Sorry," he said as he glanced around the table at his three sisters and parents.

After they prayed silently, everyone dug into the first of several special meals his mother and sisters prepared for Christmas Eve and Christmas Day. The day after Christmas would be equally as festive. On Second Christmas they would visit shut-ins and continue to celebrate the birth of Jesus. To his knowledge, Second Christmas wasn't celebrated by the English. John usually considered the extended holiday as one of the perks of being Amish. This year, he just wanted to get through the holidays and be done with it.

John eyed the loaf of cinnamon bread, pan of blueberry muffins, a potato and egg casserole, the platter of sausage and bacon, stack of pancakes, bowl of fresh fruit, and bowl of scrambled eggs. "Something for everyone," his mother always said on special occasions. John wasn't sure he could eat any of it, even though his stomach grumbled in resistance. He'd dreamed about Mae in between tossing and turning all night thinking about her. He also wondered what he would do with the Christmas present he'd made for her before he found out she didn't love him, and apparently didn't even want to talk to him.

He did his best to eat a little of the meal his sisters and mother had prepared, but after breakfast and the cleanup, his oldest sister found him out in the barn, the place he went when he wanted to be alone.

Sarah crossed over the threshold, pulling her black cape snug as she sloshed into the barn, bringing snow and ice with her. Once inside, she untied her black bonnet and shook it dry. "John, it's freezing out here, but I knew this is where you would be, assuming no one would come out here looking for you." She slapped her hands to her hips. "I know you want to be alone, but you need to at least fake some sort of festiveness for Rebecca and Anna's sake. You're so transparent, and we all know you're upset about things not working out with Mae, but you are robbing everyone else of the Christmas spirit." She paused. "Please try to remember the reason for the season."

John opened his mouth to tell Sarah to go away, but the barn door slammed shut from the wind, putting his words on pause. It was loud and jarring, and maybe a wake-up call to John. His sister was right. He chose a different approach. "I'll do *mei* best to act cheerful in front of everyone."

She walked closer to him, and with each step, her expression grew more sympathetic. "Maybe don't just *act.*" She put a hand on her chest, atop her black cape as she shivered. "Let the Holy Spirit into your heart, you might be surprised at the miracles *Gott* is capable of, including the mending of a broken heart."

Sarah leaned into him and embraced him tightly. "I *lieb* you." Then she turned and left.

"I *lieb* you too," he said barely above a whisper, glad she was out of sight before his eyes became moist.

Seconds later, he dropped to his knees, clasped his hands, and took in his surroundings, reminding him of Jesus's birth in a barn and of all the suffering the Lord's son would go through to make a place for him in Heaven.

Then he prayed that he would find the Christmas spirit . . . for real.

Even without Mae.

Chapter 7

It was late afternoon on Christmas Eve when Ruth and Henry left the Kings' house, along with Hannah's parents. Paul's parents had stopped by briefly, but they hadn't stayed long since they had several other rounds of visitation scheduled with Paul's other siblings. After waving bye to the last of their guests, Hannah closed the door, turned around, and faced her children. "I think we did pretty *gut* today."

Lillian nodded. Her youngest

daughter had fought tears on and off throughout the day, and tomorrow — Christmas Day — would be even harder. Hannah had managed to keep her emotions tucked away, in front of her houseguests but also so she wouldn't upset Ruth and Henry, or the atmosphere in general. She did her best to be festive even though she missed Paul more than ever.

Mae seemed to have the hardest time throughout the day, disappearing for long periods at a time, then returning with swollen eyes or a red face that looked previously streaked with tears. Hannah had hoped that by spilling their emotions the night before that maybe they'd released some of the grief they felt, grief that

Hannah had been hiding from her girls. As she reflected on the past six months, maybe she'd done them more harm than good by not showing her feelings. She wasn't sure if there was a right or wrong way to behave in this situation. But Mae seemed to have stepped into Hannah's shoes by trying to corral her emotions today.

Hannah wasn't sure she wouldn't have another melt-down alone this evening, but prior to that, she was going to wait until Lillian was in bed, then try to talk to Mae.

Her oldest daughter remained quiet the rest of the day. But Lillian had spurts of little girl Christmas excitement, then she would recall something about her father, and her light dimmed. Hopefully, the special gifts Hannah had made for the girls — more than usual — would bring moments of joy.

"Mae, can we talk?" Hannah posed the question after Lillian was tucked in bed upstairs.

"Um . . ." Mae was perched on the couch with her legs tucked beneath her. She lowered her legs to the floor and closed the book she was reading. "I-I was just getting ready to bathe, and —"

"Please." Hannah bit her bottom lip, willing it not to tremble. "It won't take long."

"Okay," Mae responded with little enthusiasm, almost as if she was being punished, putting her book down before crossing her arms across her chest, then sighing. "What do you want to talk about?"

Hannah wanted to tread softly, but the subject matter wasn't going to allow it. She cleared her throat. "Since your *daed* died, I wake up in the middle of the night sometimes, and I would go upstairs and check on you and Lillian. I always find you are sleeping soundly. And I know that everyone has their own way of dealing with grief, but I don't want you to feel like you must hide it. I know you've been crying a lot today."

Her daughter's mouth fell open as her eyebrows narrowed in what appeared to be anger, which was the last thing Hannah expected. "*Mamm,* prior to last night, when I burst through your bedroom door, you've been hiding your grief from everyone. You walk around like a robot just going through the motions." She held up a hand when Hannah opened her mouth to speak up. "Before you say anything, I don't mean to sound cruel, but you've been absent since *Daed* died. Lillian and I both needed that release last night, to be comforted by our *mudder* even if it was long overdue. So, if I choose not to show *mei* grief openly, I think you should respect *mei* feelings."

Hannah's heart was cracking as she blinked back tears and took a seat next to her daughter on the couch. "Mae, I'm sorry. I thought I was doing the right thing by not breaking down constantly in front of you and your sister." She lowered her head in shame. "I should have been there more for you both." Then she couldn't hold back, and she covered her face with her hands and sobbed.

"*Mamm,* please don't cry." Mae wrapped her arms around her mother. "I'm sorry. I'm sorry I said anything. I know your loss is so much worse than mine and Lillian's." Mae was crying now, but Hannah's chest tightened as she eased her daughter away.

"What? I never claimed that *mei* loss was any worse than yours and Lillian's. I know that you were shocked when he passed, that grief has plagued us all . . ." She swallowed back the growing lump in her throat as she sniffled. "We all suffered, and continue to suffer, equally. But it was *mei* mistake to pretend like everything was okay. I'm sorry. And knowing this, I wish I could go back six months because I would have done things differently."

"*Mamm,* you had *Daed* for a lot longer than Lillian and I did." She put her hand over her heart. "And you were so in *lieb.* Not everyone has what you and *Daed* had. I have plenty of friends who noticed over the years how happy you two were, often commenting that they wished their parents were like you and *Daed.*" She shook her head. "I always used to want what you and

Daed had."

Ding, ding. "What do you mean 'used to want'?" Had Hannah wrecked her daughter's life and caused her to think this way?

Mae's expression went blank as she locked eyes with Hannah. "I don't ever want to go through what you're going through." She began to cry. "To *lieb* someone so much that your heart flutters every time you're near that person, like you're floating on air, that you want to spend the rest of your life walking a foot off the ground with that person because you're so in *lieb.* I'd rather not ever *lieb* someone that way then take a chance on losing him." She lowered her head and covered her face.

Hannah's jaw had dropped somewhere along the line, so she forced her mouth closed and bit her bottom lip again. "I think it's too late, *mei lieb.* You're in *lieb* with John, aren't you?"

Mae cried harder. "*Ya,* and that's why I broke up with him. I never meant for things to get as serious as they did, and I surely didn't mean to fall in *lieb* with him. I *lieb* him so much it physically hurts sometimes." She locked eyes with Hannah again. "There are no guarantees in life, as you well know, and *Mamm* . . . I don't want to end up like you. I miss *Daed* every day, but I know you are feeling a different kind of grief. I only feel a tiny fraction of that, and I've only been seeing John for three months. What if I had married him, then lost him the way you lost *Daed*?" She lowered her head. "I couldn't survive it. That kind of loss would kill me."

"Sometimes, it feels like it did," Hannah mumbled, wishing she hadn't said what she was thinking. "Mae, you need to understand something. I would not change one thing about *mei* life. If I could have seen the future and known your father would be killed at a young age in a terrible accident, I still would have married him." Hannah gently cupped her daughter's chin and lifted her eyes to hers. "I want you to listen to me, listen carefully. There's a popular quote . . . Is it better to have *liebed* and lost or to have never *liebed* at all? I am telling you that it is better to have *liebed* and lost than to have never shared the experience. I will miss your father for the rest of *mei* life, and I will get better over time. I know this. And as time goes by, I'll be able to find joy in our memories. I'll be able to talk about him, to recall the beautiful times we had together, and laugh at recollections of his silly jokes and behavior." She offered her daughter a weak smile. "I'm just not there yet." She cupped Mae's cheek. "Please don't give up on *lieb* for fear of losing that person. We can't know the plans *Gott* has for us, but He will never forsake us. And I know that now even amid my pain and grief."

She lowered her hand to her lap, then reached for Mae's hand and squeezed it tightly between both of hers. "Don't you let John get away if you believe him to be the man of your dreams, the person you want to be with."

"I know we're young, but it feels that way, *Mamm.* Between missing him and missing *Daed . . .*" A tear slipped down Mae's cheek as she lifted her shoulders and slowly dropped them.

Hannah's heart was breaking, but it was cracking for another reason other than the death of her husband.

She squeezed Mae's hand again. "You said John told you he *liebs* you."

"*Ya,* he did," she was quick to respond.

Hannah put her hands to her face for a few seconds, taking deep breaths before she gazed at her daughter's tear-streaked face. "You're right. You're young. But so were your father and I. I knew I *liebed* your *daed* two weeks after he began courting me." She nudged Mae's shoulder with hers and winked at her. "And you know what? I told him that I *liebed* him first, after only two weeks." She chuckled. "I wish you could have seen the look on his face."

Mae cocked her head to one side as she considers what her mother is saying. "Did he say it back?"

Hannah smiled. "*Ya,* he sure did.

I felt like the luckiest young woman on the planet. I understand about walking on air, and God blessed us with a special relationship that maybe everyone doesn't have. And I'll take that over not ever having been with him, for sure." She paused. "Your father is not coming back to us. We must deal with that in our own ways. I apparently failed miserably as a mother with the way I handled it, and —"

"*Nee, Mamm.* Don't say that. You were doing what you thought best for your *kinner.* I shouldn't have said anything."

"I am thanking *Gott* that you did say something. Otherwise, you might have missed out on the *lieb* of your life."

"I didn't tell him I *liebed* him. I didn't even give him an explanation. He probably hates me by now." Mae swiped at her eyes when tears began to spill again.

"If that is the case, then he's not the right young man for you. But I seriously doubt he hates you. He might be confused or bitter because he doesn't understand why you just cut him off. He probably thinks you don't *lieb* him."

Mae shook her head. "And that is not true. I *lieb* him with all *mei* heart, but I just don't want to —"

"I know . . . end up like me." Hannah wished she could back up at least a few months, but she was going to need to make up for some lost time, and let the healing begin.

She patted her daughter on the leg. "Wait here. I have something special I want to show you, that no one has ever seen besides your father."

Mae's eyebrows lifted and she almost had a smile on her face. Maybe Christmas could be salvaged after all. And maybe Hannah could convince her daughter that true love is worth the risk of a broken heart.

Chapter 8

Mae glanced around at the gifts stacked in various places throughout the living room. Her family had exchanged presents with her aunt and uncle and grandparents, but much to Lillian's frustration, the three of them wouldn't open their gifts to each other until tomorrow after worship service. At the time when Lillian cried about it, Mae thought her mother should have made an exception to the holiday rule, but maybe keeping traditions was a better idea.

Today, they'd had ham Aunt Ruth brought, and Mae and her mother had made potato salad, baked beans, and several other side dishes that were their own established traditions — candied carrots, creamed corn, and shaved Brussels sprout with cranberries and nuts. Her grandparents brought a salted caramel pie, an apple pie, and chocolate-peppermint brownies. In keeping with tradition, Mae's mother was slow cooking a turkey overnight, and the aroma hung in the air, in a place where memories and grief collided. Mae wondered when happiness and grief would meet in the middle and become normality.

Her mother returned to the living room with a wooden box underneath her arm about the size of a shoebox. She stopped to stoke the fire, sending orange embers wafting upward, and Mae could see a gentle snow falling outside beneath the gas lamp that lit part of the front yard, which was visible from the window behind the couch.

"What's in the box?" Mae asked her mother as she sat down. She gingerly ran her hand atop the wooden surface and smiled as she turned to Mae, whose stomach twisted with anticipation.

"*Mei* memories," her mother said softly, still running her fingers along the top of the box, which Mae noticed had her parents initials carved into the wood. "I haven't opened it since your *daed* died." She swiped at a tear.

"*Mamm,* we don't have to do this. If you don't want to show me what —"

"*Ya, ya.* I do. I want you to know that every moment I spent with your father was worth the grief I am feeling now." She gently cupped Mae's cheeks and locked eyes with her before she lowered her hands and unhooked the latch.

Mae gasped when she saw some of the contents on top. "Pictures? They're not allowed." All Amish knew that. Taking photographs violated the Second Commandment that prohibited making graven images.

Her eyes widened when her mother picked up a handful of photographs. There were other things in the box, but Mae was transfixed on the top picture her mother showed her.

"We had a *rumschpringe,* you know." She chuckled. "And we didn't let it go to waste."

"Wow," Mae said softly as her mother handed her the photo. "You were so young." She laughed. "And look at those blue jeans and T-shirts." She'd never seen her parents dressed in anything besides traditional Amish attire.

"We were younger than you. Both of us were seventeen." Her mother leaned closer to Mae and rested her head on her shoulder. "He was the most handsome, wonderful, loving boy — who was almost a man — I'd ever met."

"*Ya, Daed* was handsome, for sure." She pulled the photo closer. "Aw, you're holding hands. Where was this taken?" Mae could see the corner of a house and a pond in the background. It looked familiar, but she couldn't place it in her mind.

"We were behind The Peony Inn." Everything, including Mae's heart, felt lighter when her mother laughed. "You know that Esther and Lizzie, the owners, are known matchmakers. And they were back then too. Lizzie took that picture. "Paul — your *daed* — *liebed* to fish, and once when I was visiting the widows, they asked me to take the young man down at the pond some tea. He was from another district and doing some work on the barn for Esther and Lizzie. I'd never met him before." She laughed again. "Esther took credit for introducing us. Lizzie took credit for all the times she nudged us together." She shrugged. "Their matchmaking wasn't necessary. It was *lieb* at first sight for me. And your father told me later that it was for him too."

Her mother handed her another picture of them standing in front of a movie theater, then they flipped through several photos that were taken in restaurants. All the Amish Mae knew frequented restaurants, but she'd only known a few teenagers in their running around period who had gone to a movie. Mae secretly hoped she would be able to do so before she was baptized, and apparently, her parents had seen a movie together.

"Who took these pictures?" Mae knew lots of Amish folks who had cell phones, but she was pretty sure selfies were not popular twenty years ago.

"We had a regular old camera, the kind where you had to go have the photos developed. We would ask people to take pictures of us, and no one knew we were Amish since we were wearing *Englisch* clothes." She giggled. "Except for Lizzie when she took that picture of us at

The Peony Inn, but she's always been a tad nontraditional."

"Where's this?" Mae eyed a faded photo, unable to make out the object in the picture.

"Jug Rock."

Mae pulled the picture closer to her face until the image came into focus and she recognized the only freestanding table rock formation east of the Mississippi. "In Shoals, right?"

"*Ya.* It's where we had our first kiss. No one was around to take a picture of us . . ." She laughed, which was becoming a magical melody Mae had missed so much. "Nor did we want anyone around. So, we took a picture of the rock."

"*Ach,* look at this." She pulled out

a string with a tiny cross, a necklace. "We each had one, but your *daed* lost his on a rollercoaster."

Now it was Mae who roared with laughter. "I cannot even imagine you and *Daed* on a rollercoaster." She handed the picture to her mother. "Well, I haven't been putting *mei rumschpringe* to *gut* use. I need to get busy."

"We did have a lot of fun . . . but only for three months. Then we were baptized and married a month later."

Her mother set the photos and necklace aside and began going through the other items in the box, each with a story or memory attached to it. And her mother smiled the entire time, an occasional tear, but there were fond recollections, laughter, and all Mae could think was *I have* mei *mom back.*

Would it last? She didn't know. But, at this very moment, she wanted her mother to know how she felt. Aside from the wonderful smell of turkey cooking, the fire crackling, the light snowfall that continued, Mae wanted her mom to know how special this Christmas was to her, despite the void.

"Mamm?"

Her mother turned to her, eyes glistening, but not from tears. There was a glow about her that Mae hadn't seen in a long time. *"Ya?"*

"*Danki.* This is the best Christmas present you could have ever given me." A tear rolled down her cheek, and her mother's soft thumb was there to gently wipe it away.

"You're welcome, sweet child of mine." Her mother closed the box and hooked the latch, then held it against her chest. "There will still be tears, but *mei* memories will sustain me, and I promise to be more transparent with *mei* feelings. I want you to do the same." She smiled. "I'm glad we opened this box together."

"Me too." She threw her arms around her mom. "I *lieb* you so much."

"I *lieb* you, too, and your *daed liebed* you and Lillian very much also. He would want us to be happy." Then she eased away, pressed her lips together, and tapped Mae on the nose with her finger, grinning. "Now, don't you let that boy get away. Do you hear me?"

Mae nodded, then thanked God for the wonderful Christmas Eve she'd been blessed with.

John struggled to keep his sister's advice in the forefront of his mind — *remember the reason for the season.* The service was being held at The Peony Inn, and thankfully so since the large house was roomy enough for everyone to have a place to eat indoors. It was another smaller service, though, due to the weather, John assumed.

But even the aroma of a simmering meal and the festive decorations throughout the home didn't propel his emotions in the right direction. Sitting through Christmas Day worship with a clear view of Mae and her family pulled his mind away from the service. By the time the bishop wrapped things up, John realized he'd been so preoccupied that he had stumbled his way through the prayers and scripture readings without retaining much of what was said.

His mood shifted when the service was over, and Mae asked if she could talk to him after the meal. He nodded with too much enthusiasm. After she'd walked away, he accepted the possibility that her wanting to chat with him might not have anything to do with how she felt about him. It might be something totally unrelated, but he couldn't help but feel hopeful.

Lizzie and Esther, owners of the inn, along with the other women, had prepared a lavish display. The bishop allowed things to be fancier during the holidays, and The Peony Inn glowed with Christmas spirit. White cloths covered the additional tables set up in the large dining room, all with holly wreaths around candelabras with red candles. One table was against the wall and filled with beautifully decorated desserts.

Still . . . it was the longest meal of John's life, but when Mae finally approached him, he couldn't get up fast enough. Most folks were in the dining room still eating and chatting.

"Can we talk? Maybe in the den over by the fireplace? It will be more private." Mae held up a finger. "I just need to do something quickly. Can you meet me there in about two minutes?"

"Uh, *ya.*" John's mind scrambled with confusion. Mae was chipper, fueling his hope that whatever she had to say would be related to their relationship, but she'd been clear about how she felt about him.

As the fire crackled nearby, sprawling orange flames warming the space, John waited for what felt longer than two minutes. Three of the elders were in the far corner of the room, but they were in deep conversation.

"Sorry, it took longer than I thought," she said as sidled up next to him, the closest he'd been to her in a long time. He breathed in the familiar scent of her lavender shampoo and lotion. "I had to take care of something. But . . ." She lowered her head, and when she looked up, she had tears in her eyes.

"What's wrong?" His hope was chipping off like pieces of an already broken heart.

"I'm sorry for something else too." She glanced at the three men in the corner, their heads still buried in a circle of conversation, then she threw her arms around him and hung on tightly. "I *lieb* you," she whispered in his ear. "I *lieb* you with all *mei* heart."

He eased her away and locked eyes with her. "But you didn't say —"

"I know, I know. I was so scared. Terrified of losing you. We are grieving about losing *mei daed,* but I've watched *mei mudder* grieve in a way I didn't know was possible, and I *lieb* you so much that I didn't ever want to feel that way. But *mei mudder* convinced me that it is better to have *liebed* and lost than to never *lieb* at all. And if you'll still have me, I —"

"Still have you?" John didn't think he could smile any broader as he cupped her cheeks with both hands. "You are the *lieb* of *mei* life. I'm sure of it."

"And I feel the same way, John." Mae's face, illuminated by the glow of twinkling lights atop the mantle of the fireplace, shone with truth and sincerity. The warmth of the Christmas spirit finally found him as the chipped pieces of his broken heart began to mend.

He kissed her again before he eased away and said, "I made something for you before you stopped talking to me. I almost didn't bring it, but I felt a nudge I couldn't ignore and put it in *mei* buggy at the last minute."

She lowered her gaze. "I-I'm afraid I don't have a gift for you."

He cupped her cheeks again until she finally looked up. "Your *lieb* is the best Christmas present ever.

Nothing can top that." He held up one finger. "Wait here." Then he dashed out the front door of the inn without putting on his coat. Luckily it had stopped snowing, and he grabbed the gift bag he'd put in the backseat.

Breathless, he ran back to the house and met her beside the fireplace, and the warmth of the fire spread to his heart as he handed her the gift. A few more people had gathered in the living room, but the fireplace at the inn was enormous, and no one paid much attention to them off to one side of it.

Smiling, Mae removed the tissue from the bag, then gasped when she saw what was inside. "*Ach*, John."

"I carved the box." He eyed the two hearts he had whittled into the front of the cedar, barely crossing over each other.

She gingerly undid the latch and ran her hand across the white felt he'd glued inside.

"Our hearts will always be as one." Clutching the box, she leaned up on her toes and kissed him the way he remembered, filled with passion . . . and love. His heart was full. He could feel eyes on them, but he didn't care. Mae loved him, and that was all that mattered.

"Best Christmas ever," he said between kisses. "I'll remember this moment for the rest of *mei* life."

"Me too." She kissed him again just as Lizzie came flying around the corner.

Lizzie, the petite co-owner of The Peony Inn, stood in the entryway to the den with her husband looking over her shoulder and strands of gray hair flying loose from beneath her prayer covering. "I'm sorry! I'm late!" She held up a mobile phone and addressed Mae. "Am I late?"

"*Nee,* you are just in time." Then she kissed John again as Lizzie snapped several pictures.

"Mission accomplished," Lizzie's tall husband said from behind her. "Let's let these two young people be alone."

They were hardly alone. More folks had come into the den. Photos weren't allowed, and public affection was frowned upon. But out of the corner of his eye, John caught the bishop slightly smiling. He supposed it was hard not to be joyous, even if rules were broken, when love abounded.

John looked at Mae, grinning. "What was all that about?"

"I'll explain it to you someday." Mae winked.

He pulled her close, kissed her again, and thanked God for this Christmas gift. For Mae. And for the prospect of many more Christmases together.

"Merry Christmas, Mae." John gazed into her eyes, his heart full.

She smiled. "Merry Christmas to you, too, John."

Epilogue

Many years later . . .

Mae slipped into her nightgown, fluffed her pillows, then slid into bed next to her husband. "It was a wonderful, blessed Christmas," she said as she lowered the light on the lantern just a little bit.

"*Ya,* it was. We sure had a houseful." John smiled. "I counted twenty-five."

"And it will be twenty-six in a couple of months." Mae smiled as she thought about their family —

six children, seventeen grandchildren, and soon-to-be great-grandchild.

Then, as was tradition, she reached for the small red suitcase that John had already retrieved from the closet and put on the edge of the bed. She opened it up and took out the cedar box he'd given her that Christmas so long ago. Her mother had long since passed, but Mae had carried on her tradition. There were baby shoes, baby clothes Mae had made, silver rattles, pictures their children and grandchildren had drawn or painted, cards for special occasions, and a host of other memorabilia they'd collected throughout their lives — including a picture standing in front of a movie theater. And, of course, the photos that Lizzie had taken of them by the fireplace at The Peony Inn.

"Look at us," she said softly. "We were so young."

"And so in *lieb.*" John leaned closer and gazed at the picture before he kissed her.

She had to believe her mother was smiling down on them from heaven. And her father too. Mae and John had never shown anyone the contents of their box. Maybe one day, she or her husband would be sharing it with their children and grandchildren. *Or maybe not.*

John chuckled. "There are a lot of stories represented in that box."

Mae smiled at her husband as she

recalled their long lives, the adventures they'd had, especially when they'd embraced their *rumschpringe* for all it was worth before being baptized and getting married.

"We've been blessed," she said as she put the lid on the large box.

"*Ya,* we have."

Her husband put the box back in the red suitcase, closed it, then put it back in the closet for safekeeping. They would continue to add pertinent items to their memory box, but they wouldn't go through it again until next Christmas, the way they'd been doing for sixty-two years.

"Merry Christmas, Mae."

She smiled and thanked God for

the life she'd been blessed with. "Merry Christmas, John."

Yumasetti Casserole

Ingredients:

2 pounds ground beef
1 onion, chopped
12 oz. egg noodles
2 cups frozen peas
2 (10.5 oz.) cans cream of mushroom soup
2 (10.5 oz.) cans cream of chicken soup
1 cup sour cream
2 cups bread crumbs, crumbled

3 T. butter, melted

Instructions:

Cook the noodles as directed on the package;

Brown the ground beef with the onion, then drain the fat;

Combine the noodles, beef, peas, soups, and sour cream in a large bowl. Pour mixture into a greased 9×13 baking dish;

Toss breadcrumbs with the melted butter in a small bowl, then sprinkle on top of casserole;

Cover the dish with foil and bake in a 350 degrees oven for 25-30 minutes;

Uncover and bake for 15-20 minutes until lightly brown on top.

(Serves 10-12 people)

Onion Patties

Ingredients:

1 cup all-purpose flour
2 tsp. baking powder
2 tsp. sugar
1/2 tsp. salt
1/4 tsp. black pepper
2 T. cornmeal
2.5 cups onions, chopped
1 cup milk
1/2 cup cooking oil

Instructions:

Using a whisk, combine the flour, sugar, baking powder, salt, pepper, and cornmeal in a large bowl, then mix in chopped onions. Pour in milk and mix with a spoon.

Heat oil and carefully drop spoonfuls into hot oil. Cook on one side until brown, then flip to brown the other side.

Add additional salt, pepper, or other seasonings.

Pickled Eggs with Beets

Ingredients:

2 (15 oz.) cans whole beets
12 hard-boiled eggs, peeled
1 cup water
1 cup sugar
1 cup cider vinegar

Instructions:

Drain beets and reserve 1 cup of the juice;

Put beets and eggs in a 2-qt. glass jar;

In a small saucepan, bring the sugar, water, vinegar, and reserved beet juice to a boil;

Poor mixture over beets and eggs and let cool;

After covering tightly, refrigerate for 24 hours before serving.

MAE'S AMISH CHICKEN (CORN) SOUP

Ingredients:

1 cup shredded carrots
2 celery ribs, chopped
1 medium onion, chopped
2 pounds chicken breasts, cubed
3 chicken bouillon cubes
1 tsp. salt
1/4 tsp. pepper
12 cups of water

2 cups egg noodles, uncooked
2 (14-3/4 oz) cans cream-style corn
1/4 cup butter
Nutmeg to taste (Mae's secret ingredient)

Instructions:

Combine first eight ingredients in a Dutch oven and bring to a slow boil;

Reduce heat and simmer, uncovered, until chicken is done and vegetables are tender, about 30-40 minutes;

Stir in the noodles, corn, and butter. Cook until noodles are tender, about 10-15 minutes, stirring occasionally;

Add salt and pepper to taste.

Hannah and Mae's Shaved Brussels Sprouts with Nuts and Cranberries

Ingredients:

Cooking spray (your preference)
1 pound Brussels sprouts
1/4 cup reduced sugar dried cranberries
1/8 cup pine nuts
1/2 teaspoon salt
1/4 teaspoon black pepper
1/4 teaspoon garlic powder
pepper flakes to taste (optional)

Instructions:

Shave or thinly slice the Brussels sprouts (or use pre-shaved);

Spray a frying pan with oil spray and sauté the Brussels sprouts over medium heat until they start to soften, about 5 minutes;

Add the pine nuts and dried cranberries and sauté for another 2-3 minutes;

Season with salt, black pepper, garlic powder, and the optional red pepper flakes, if desired;

Remove from heat and serve right away.

Hannah and Mae's Candied Carrots

Ingredients:

1 lb. carrots, peeled and sliced
3 T. brown sugar
2 T. butter
1/8 tsp. pepper
1/4 tsp. Salt

1 T. parsley, chopped

Instructions:

Combine 1 cup water and carrots in a large pot. Bring to a simmer, then cook for 8 minutes or until tender;

Drain the water, return pot to medium heat;

Add the brown sugar, butter, salt, and pepper;

Cook until butter and sugar have melted and carrots are coated in the glaze — about 3 minutes;

Sprinkle with parsley, then serve.

ACKNOWLEDGMENTS

My sincerest thanks goes to God for continuing to bless me with stories to tell.

Janet Murphy, you are an amazing assistant, marketing strategist, research pro, proof reader . . . wearing too many hats to list here. Much love and thanks for your keen insight about the industry, and especially for your friendship.

Much thanks to my dear friend and editor, Audrey Wick. I couldn't do this without you! Xo

To my sweet Hubby, Patrick, I love you. Thank you for the umpteenth time for doing life with me.

I have a wonderful street team who helps promote my books. You gals aren't just huge readers, but you are sincere, dedicated, and sweet ladies. Thank you from the bottom of my heart.

To Natasha Kern, thank you for setting me on the right professional path and for our friendship, which I cherish.

Thank you to my family and friends who continue to support me on this wild and fabulous ride. Love you all.

ABOUT THE AUTHOR

Bestselling and award-winning author **Beth Wiseman** has sold over 2.5 million books. She is the recipient of the coveted Holt Medallion, a two-time Carol Award winner, and has won the Inspirational Reader's Choice Award three times. Her books have been on various bestseller lists, including CBD, CBA, ECPA, and *Publishers Weekly.* Beth and her husband are empty nesters enjoying country life in south central Texas.

The employees of Thorndike Press hope you have enjoyed this Large Print book. All our Thorndike Large Print titles are designed for easy reading, and all our books are made to last. Other Thorndike Press Large Print books are available at your library, through selected bookstores, or directly from us.

For information about titles, please call:

(800) 223-1244

or visit our website at:

gale.com/thorndike